MOGZILLA

London Sink

First published by Mogzilla in 2018
Printed in the UK
ISBN: 9781906132378

The *London Deep* series follows the adventures of Jemima Mallard: the rule-breaking daughter of a policeman whose mother heads up an underground organisation called Father Thames. Told in a mixture of words and comic art, the story unfolds to reveal how the failure of the 'Climate Upgrade' wrecked the environment and drove young people and grown-ups apart.

'This is a terrifically atmospheric page-turning adventure told through words and comic art...' – *Lovereading.co.uk*

www.londondeep.co.uk

Recap

This series is set in the near future in a flooded London where rival police forces for kids and grown-ups compete to keep the peace. London was flooded when an attempt to fix global warming – *The Climate Upgrade* – went badly wrong. Exactly what happened is long forgotten.

Jemima Mallard's father is a Chief Inspector in the APD (Adult Police Department).

In book 1, *London Deep*, Jem breaks so many laws that even her father can't help her. Arrested by a YPD (Youth Police Department) officer called Nick, she made a bargain. In exchange for a pardon, she helped the YPD track down a criminal organisation called *Father Thames,* only to discover that her own mother was one of its leaders.

In book 2, *Father Thames,* Londoners were stunned when armed invaders appeared in warships. The strangers demanded that London send them workers for their 'Stormfather'. But the Stormfather turned out to be just an ancient wind turbine. With the help of an islander called Harfleur and leading Father Thames member Shami, Jem and her father managed to get the wind farm generating valuable electricity again. Shami steals a mask that belonged to the Islanders' mad leader and sends a signal asking to be picked up.

In book 3, *Threadneedle,* Jem returns to London to find that a deadly plague called 'threadneedle' has broken out. Jem's ex-boyfriend Nick and her father are both infected. Jem recruits a team of mercenaries to rescue Mallard from a 'safeguarding' facility.

Jem's mother has discovered a treatment for the deadly virus and helps Nick. But despite Jem's pleas she refuses to share the cure with Jem's father.

Prologue

Six hours after Shami sent the signal, they came to the stormfather island and found her.

Shami's plan was to head back to London, deliver the mask and collect the reward from the bargers. But that was before the outbreak of 'threadneedle' – a deadly disease that swept through London like a medieval plague.

Chapter 1: Electricity

The pre-dawn fog hung around the mech's legs like diesel smoke in the bilges. Ragnar perched on the mech — an overweight parrot on the great machine's shoulder. The harpoon in his hand had cruel barbs. This was no 'poon gun but an old fashioned lance with a bloody history. Fray grinned up at

Ragnar as the gondola glided past. Even by barger standards, Fray's boat was built to turn heads. With its 2 metre high bronze totem shaped like a venetian gondolier, Fray's *Ozymandias* was arguably the most ridiculous looking craft west of the Thames Barrier reef. But Ragnar wasn't smiling as it came towards him.

"Halt!" roared Ragnar indignantly, peering down from his perch atop the seized steel giant. The mech had been powered down long ago, but a mechanical exoskeleton lends anyone an air of authority. Now it served as a kind of armoured toll booth, bestriding the river like a rusting Colossus.

Fray grinned an easy grin as the gondola slid towards the steel sentinel.

Fray ignored Ragnar's demand for money and sailed straight for the gap between the giant mech's legs. He pointed the prow of the gondola at the twin 'sink' towers. They overlooked the waters where the bargers moored their ever expanding flotilla of boats.

The history of the bargers and their kingdom was long and bloody. But Fray paid as much attention to history as a reed in the marsh pays to the wind. The history of the bargers was in books but like most men, (his father being a notable exception) Fray couldn't read more than a few words. Reading and writing was women's work.

Beyond the sink towers lay the great fence with its rich pickings. The Agreement forbade the bargers from leaving their kingdom. Rules were made to be broken – and when you broke the law you had to pay the Ferryman.

Ragnar brandished the lance that had stopped the hearts of 30 whales and repeated his demand for payment. Fray looked up at him, struggling to maintain his smile as the boat drew closer.

Ragnar raised the harpoon. Fray flicked a switch and the green eyes of the gondola's totem lit up. Roaring and cursing, Ragnar threw the lance. But Fray had already activated the gondola's defences. Gears whirred as a protective cage slid out from the totem's outstretched arms. The harpoon wedged itself harmlessly in the steel mesh.

Ragnar yanked the cable furiously but the harpoon barb was wedged tight. The unfortunate Ragnar began to yell half-formed curses about there being a reckoning for this but while he was shouting, the cable was playing out behind the departing gondola. Fray hit the throttle and the boat's illegal fossil fuel engine roared into life. Inductors whirred and it shot forward like a cork out of a bottle. Bellowing wild curses, Ragnar fumbled with the carabiner on his belt, trying to unclip the cable. But it was too late...

'The Ferryman must be paid' – went the saying. But the old patriarch with his laws held no sway over Fray. It was not a rejection of the bargers' ancient code, it was simpler than that: Fray was the Ferryman's son. And as he liked to remind everyone, he'd been paying all of his life.

The gondola surged through the water dragging Ragnar behind it like a reluctant child on his first waveboarding lesson. Fray had grown up with Ragnar – he used protect him from the clans. Even the meanest clan rats dropped their shuriken when they found out they were facing the Ferryman's son. That was before Ragnar had filled out. Whether it was 'aftermarket' genes or a growth spurt, Ragnar didn't need protecting now. Still waving, Fray cut the cable. Sighing, he picked up his harpoon gun and shot a float towards the sinking man. Fray didn't want the big guy to drown. There were enough sunken hazards in the Thames already.

Fray flicked the wheel and the gondola veered left to avoid a collision with *The Wounded Siren*.

The *Siren* was the last boat in the world that Fray wanted to smash into. Although most Londoners cursed all bargers as thieves and river rats, the bargers fought each other like the highland clans of old. *The Wounded Siren* belonged to the head of the Kirkless family: the oldest crew on the river and certainly the ugliest. Their leader, Dadder Kirkless, paid public tribute to The Ferryman – grudgingly. But in private his folk were on the hunt for grievances. The Ferryman had given the bargers peace but it was a thin scab over their differences. The Kirklesses wanted to pick at that scab. They were itching for trouble.

"Trying to swamp us Fray?" screamed a terrier-faced guard.

"Just passing," called Fray apologetically, struggling to keep his balance.

Fray ignored them and glided serenely on. Popular opinion had it that bargers took to fighting like sharks take to a blood slick. They fought duals, they carried blades and they threw shuriken stars at each other for fun. 'Barger frisbee' – that was called. But to the disappointment of his father, Fray was built for peace not war. He'd survived countless years of blood-feuds and he wasn't going to answer any challenges today.

The sink towers loomed closer. They'd been called 'sink' estates in the days before the flood, he remembered. Fray had been to the Pastkeeper's Palace once. But he'd tuned out when his dadder had started talking about history – like everyone else he was only interested in seeing the robots.

As the lights of *The Wounded Siren* turned to a string of orange dots, Fray checked his equipment. His 'fishing line' was a long copper cable with a magnetic hook. Fray raised the harpoon gun, took aim and squeezed the trigger. The cable whizzed high into the mist towards the fence. A spatter of white sparks told Fray that it had found its target. Fray hooked up his battery and the needle twitched before settling on the 20 ampere per hour mark. Fishing requires time and patience and Fray was fishing for his favourite brand of electricity – other peoples'! In the wind-up world of post upgrade London, power was in short supply. They'd got by for years on renewables. Wind turbines would keep you topped up, as long the wind was blowing. Solar power was better – you didn't even need bright sun to get the current flowing. But London had been living on patched up solar for 70 years now. To make the photovoltaic panels you needed rare metals like cadmium and iridium. Over the years the panels had failed and could not be replaced.

That made a fishing trip to the fence an increasingly attractive proposition. You'd pick a foggy night and slide up to the fence nice and slow, hook up a cable and fill your boots.

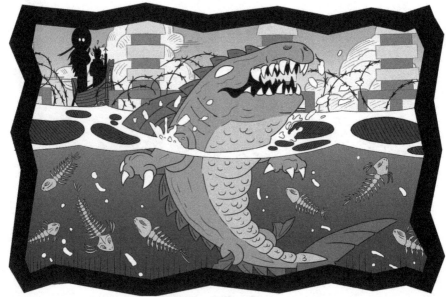

There was one fly in the ointment – when you drained the fence, the power level went down. And the fence was there for a reason – to keep sharks and other nasties out of London's waters.

The waiting was the worst part. It would take hours to get a full charge. Like the sharks on the other side of the wire, Fray was not born for stillness. He craved physical activity to stop his mind getting 'choppy'. He played with the broken kit in order to pass the time. Suddenly, a metallic voice broke the silence.

Fray had to think fast. The drone was an evil piece of carbon fibre – from the soulless school of design that dictators drooled over as they swiped through the pages of their 'Death Tech' catalogues.

Fray had junked plenty of drones like this before. The trouble was that the drone was flat sided. It had been built flat in order to minimise its radar profile. But that also meant it was hard to hit with a 'poon if you were side on to it. Fray wondered if the warning about seekers was a trick. Rumour had it that the APD were running low of heat seeking missiles after a technician dropped a blowtorch in the armoury.

In order to destroy the drone he'd have to get it moving. Fray snapped the control panel up. It was time to unclip and go. He clicked the button and the totem's eyes blinked on.

Chapter 2: On

Jem winced as she put the new YPD badge on. Unicorns were noble beasts, she thought. Surely they do not deserve this.

Urgh!

Jem needed another YPD job like a fish needs second hooking. So what had convinced her to sign up for a second tour of duty? Money. Briefly, she'd been rich. But she'd exchanged her share in the Stormfather island to hire a team of mercs to rescue her father. They'd snatched Mallard from a 'safeguarding' centre but her father was infected with the threadneedle disease. Treatments were being developed but progress was slow. Mallard was no longer at death's door, but he was still in its general vicinity. Her thoughts went to their last meeting.

Typical father, 20 years service, thought Jem, and then he retires without telling me. But the killer blow was that the APD had tricked her father out of his benefits. Mallard had got the threadneedle disease after his official retirement date. After he'd left the force. Antitox – the new medicine that kept it at bay – was the most expensive drug available. Jem's mother, River could have helped, but she was not the helping kind.

Still waters run deep, but they also run cold. Jem wasn't going to forgive her mother in a hurry. River had nearly got her dad and her ex-boyfriend killed. Jem often thought about her dad and wrote to him. She thought about Nick too sometimes.

On some subconscious level, Jem probably knew that joining the YPD – an organisation that her mother hated with an oceanic depth – was a deliberate act of defiance designed to wound her. How does a girl pay for her sick father's meds? Have tazor, will travel. Jem loathed the YPD, but it was a solid payer. It was still a year till Jem's 16th birthday, and that meant 12 months of salary payments.

It had seemed to make sense as she signed the papers. But out on the river, Jem didn't know if she could hack it. Where did the YPD get officers like her new partner Hanzi from? Was there a production line of officious kids who liked ordering other people around? She was stuck with a new YPD recruit with an itchy trigger finger – or an itchy ticket writing finger in Hanzi's case.

Jem spotted a small dark shape whizzing low through the fog. She looked again but the object was lost against the background of slate grey waves.

"An APD drone," said Hanzi excitedly.

"Yay," said Jem sarcastically, easing back into her chair. She wasn't sure she could stick another 12 months of this. "I'll tell Kontrol we're standing down."

"You don't decide whether we standing down or not!" snapped Hanzi, pushing his hand in front of the mic. "You don't outrank me."

"Sorry to sink your flagship Admiral, but if that's an APD drone then this is their crime scene," said Jem, wondering at how jaded her own voice sounded.

Hanzi looked like a dog that had lost its bone.

"Standing down?" he gasped. "No! Not before the age of the perp has been positively identified."

Hanzi turned the handle on the transponder tracker, winding power into the system. Every YPD boat had a tracker display for reading age ID chips. A blue light meant the perp's ID chip was under 16 and a red light meant over.

"Fill!" said Hanzi in frustration. Suddenly, his face lit up.

20

Chapter 3: Beat the clock

Fray pulled the probe out of his arm and bit down on the gag.

The ID chips were implanted at the back of your neck, but Fray's had been relocated to his left shoulder. It was a cheap graft job – the sort of surgery that the patchers from Harley St used to go in for. The act of removing a chip was a crime. What Fray was doing now could earn him five years in the YPD's Bloody Tower, or whichever threadneedle infested maximum security 'safeguarding centre' the APD were using to hold their prisoners these days.

Fray carefully guided the probe into the flesh of his shoulder. The medication had taken the edge off the pain but digging around in your own flesh felt wrong. And it hurt like hell. A green light and a whirring sound told him that the probe had locked onto his ID chip. He yanked hard, gasped in agony and released the trigger before dropping the chip into a pouch marked with the word *Doritos*.

Inside this ancient silver-lined bag, the ID chip's signals could not be detected. It was something his father called a Faraday pouch. He would keep the chip for later inside the faded packet. He might need to change his age again at some time in the future.

The drone lowered itself on a whirl of rotors. Cold mist was blown into his face. Fray smiled.

"The APD have got no authority over me," he said politely. The drone's motors whirred, and its camera scanned his face.

"Scan me again if you don't believe me," said Fray smiling.

"Thank you for your cooperation," said the plastic voice of the drone. The nearest YPD vessel has been notified and is on route to assist with your offence."

"Losers!!!!" thought Fray, clutching his left shoulder as the drone whirred above him. The gauge on the battery was reading 7 out of a possible 9 bars. Not a full recharge but he wasn't going to hang around and get arrested. It was time to hit it and quit. Two button pushes activated the illegal but pleasing petrol motor and the gondola reared up on its hydrofoil. It sprang forward, the green lights from the totem's eyes cutting holes in the mist.

Fray let out his trademark "Yeehaaaa!" but the victorious whoop died on his lips when he spotted the YPD Krewboat.

Chapter 4: Half charged

HANZI LET OUT A WHOOP OF JOY. "Yeeehaaaa!" Jem stiffled a sigh. No doubt Hanzi thought he 'owned' this dumb whooping thing but half the kids in London were doing it. The fad made Jem feel ancient. She eased back the throttle as the boat skipped over the water like an armoured skimming stone. As Hanzi had pointed out – their new U19 was the most advanced boat that the YPD had ever built.

"It's 25 percent lighter than the previous model," said Hanzi, who'd read the spec till he could recite it like a mantra.

"It's half the size of the old ones," said Jem.

"They designed it smaller for manoeuvrability," said Hanzi proudly.

"They made it smaller because they're running out of resin for the fabricator machines," sighed Jem.

Hanzi knew she had a point. It was getting harder and harder to 'fab' stuff these days. Hanzi gestured towards a fog bank and Jem hit the spotlights. An arch of bright white light appeared.

"Stop barger!!" called Hanzi, shaking his tiny fist. If he had a tazor, he'd probably fire it, thought Jem. She shot him a stormy look and wondered whether it was worth engaging in an argument. But her father – DCI Mallard – had brought her up to speak her mind.

"How do you know he's a barger? Besides, not all bargers are criminals..." she was about to say. But Jem's voice was lost under the rising noise of the engine and Hanzi wasn't listening anyway.

The barger's boat was fast but he'd made a mistake turning towards the Sink Towers. Hanzi knew every mud bank and channel of these waters as well as he knew the U19 manual. The YPD boat made a fast turn and shot after the fleeing gondola. Now they had the barger pinned down in a narrow channel which ended in a sandbar.

Hanzi shot an uneasy glance at Jem. The bargers had a reputation for random violence. Ruined towers loomed out of the mist. Seagulls wheeled above the dead calm of the dark water.

"Cut your engine!" ordered Hanzi again, trying to calm the tremor in his voice. It had gone up a semi-tone in the last three sentences.

"He's a barger remember," said Jem earnestly.

Hanzi peered out over the grey water. The red eyes of the totem cut through the gloom. "Those guys come prepared," continued Jem. "I expect he's probably sharpening his shuriken and untieing his croc as we speak."

Hanzi went slightly paler at the thought of this image.

"Don't go in half charged," said Jem. "That's all I'm saying."

Jem looked at the holster where Hanzi's side-arm was still sitting. She knew exactly why he hadn't drawn it. She was playing with him.

"There's a problem," said Hanzi, drawing the tazor from its holster. The problem was obvious.

Hanzi eyed the barger in silence. The powerjacker looked big for his age. Jem saw the fear in her partner's eyes. Hanzi was the proud type. She knew it was wrong to shame him like this.

26

Jem fired at the totem and sparks railed out across the deck. The force blasted the barger overboard. A corona of blue sparks lit up the gondola and the totem's red eyes blinked out.

Jem fished out a life jacket and threw it to the barger, who was shivering as he trod water.

"Seriously," said Hanzi. "I need a decent battery. I've got some cred coins saved up."

"I thought you were getting that sorted last night?"

"Nah!" said Hanzi. "That fell through. The barger never showed."

Jem gave him a withering look. Her new partner hadn't been issued with a battery pack, which meant that either the YPD thought that it would be a waste of electricity, or they thought that he might zap himself in the head. The tazors was supposed to be a 'non-lethal' weapon. It was even less lethal when it had no batteries. Jem reached into her pocket, sighed and took out her spare battery pack.

"I got this on the Stormfather island," she said. "You can pay me back later. Just don't fire unless my life is under threat."

"Thanks partner," said Hanzi, serving her a cheesy grin.

"Help get him aboard," said Jem. "And don't call me partner."
Jem got the 'perp' back onto the YPD boat as Hanzi glared at him like a fish-stall cat. He was itching to interrogate his new prisoner. Fray calmly protested his innocence.

"Some kind of mistake officers?" he said in an easy drawl.

"Cable him!' snapped Hanzi, searching his pockets for cable ties.

"Is that really necessary?" asked Fray politely.

"It's procedure," said Hanzi by way of an explanation.

Tiring of waiting, Jem passed Hanzi her own bag of cable ties.

Fray sighed. He'd managed to ditch some of his 'fishing' gear over the side, but a thorough search of the gondola would reveal a number of surprises. One thing was for certain, he wasn't going to let these two take him to the Bloody Tower for questioning. All he needed was an half a chance.

With their catch landed, Jem set a course parallel with the fence, towards the beckoning lights of inner London.

Chapter 5: Candidate

The journey from the Stormfather Island back to London was only supposed to take a few days. Because of the outbreak of the threadneedle plague, it had taken Shami months to recover the mask.

"Give a man a mask and he will show his true face," wasn't that what the Ferryman had said? It was a quote from a dead Irishman. Shami hadn't given it much thought until now. Put a mask on, and a person was free to act however she liked – free from shame or accountability. If no one can see your face, you can do anything you like.

She turned her attention to the masked pair who'd picked her up. What made young men want to play at being machines? The glowing red eyes were a nice touch. She wondered where the eyes drew their power from. They didn't seem to need winding up. Shami strolled up the gangplank and along the deck to the wooden door. Gripping the mask a little too tightly, she went directly to the biggest cabin.

"Welcome to my 'bin" said the old man. Bin meant 'cabin'. It was the one word of barger slang that everyone knew – like 'apples and pears' in classical cockney. Shami's gran said she'd never met a Londoner who said 'apples and pears' instead of stairs. Was the old man mocking her?

The robots entered the room behind Shami. Robot one was eager, practically trying to snatch the bundle from her hands. The old man gave him a reproachful look. Bad robot!

The Ferryman rose from his chair. On his desk stood an idol with an ornate gold base. It was the kind of flashy trinket that bargers couldn't resist. The Ferryman twisted the head of the idol. A mechanism let out a solid clunk. The wooden wall slid upwards to reveal a hidden door. Lighting the way with a krill oil lamp, the Ferryman beckoned for Shami to follow him through to the secret room beyond. What Shami saw next, made her shudder. The room was full of masks.

31

Chapter 6: Hateful

Jem wondered if there was some kind of YPD training course for annoying your prisoners. She steered the boat through the mist as she heard snatches of Hanzi's interrogation. Phrases like: "we know how to deal with you,' and "no one lies to the YPD," and "thieving bargers – stealing our sparks!" drifted over the hum of the motor. Jem sighed. No wonder the prisoner was keeping his mouth shut. Rounding a bend in the river, she was greeted by an unexpected sight. A large ferryboat – *The Wounded Siren* – was sinking by the bow.

Jem stared at the scene, her eyes wider than ever. The oversized barger boat was tipping into the water A string of smaller craft had come to its aid. But it was too late to save *The Wounded Siren*.

"Hostile vessels heading our way," called Hanzi.

The man with the crocodile didn't look too impressed with Hanzi's threat. His companion scowled. The two boats edged towards each other. As if on cue, the croc snarled and snapped at Hanzi. Instinctively, the kid stepped back in fear. A gust of wind blew his YPD hat from his head. The thin man smiled a close-lipped smile and let the croc slip off its leash. Noiselessly, it slid off the boat, seized Hanzi's hat in its jaws and glared at the YPD with black ice eyes.

The croc bit down hard. Teeth as long as carpentry nails speared the cap's brim, piercing the YPD logo. Tymon Kirkless grinned and Jem fought the urge to join in: Hanzi's silly hat deserved to die.

Jem wondered how Tymon was controlling the croc. Was it voice control? Some sort of transmitter on the croc's collar perhaps?

"What's your drift lads?" asked Hanzi. He'd probably been on a course about barger culture and was trying to 'engage', she thought.

"That's not happening!" said Jem. "But you can keep my partner's hat and interrogate that if you like."

This drew a faint smile from Tymon, but not from his brother.

"Not you YPD. Uncle wants Fray. On account of him sinking the Siren," said the grim faced Symon.

"Why does Uncle Aeson want with me? This isn't my work," protested Fray. "Why would I want a clan war?"

The man's stare had a cold intensity. He looked at Fray in the way that a sea hawk eyes a young rat on its first trip from the nest.

Tymon Kirkless held up the offending 'fletch' – a wooden arrow with a broad metal tip like a shark's tooth. A fletch could be fired from a spring-loaded fletchette gun. Some preferred a miniature version worn on the wrist. The steel fletch tips were valuable in their own right. They were sometimes used instead of money if chip coins were in short supply. You'd cut a mark into the feathers to show that the dart belonged to you. The other way was to cast your mark into the steel tip. And this is what Symon was pointing at now.

"That can't be mine," protested Fray, eying his own runes on the fletch in disbelief. "Why would I want to kill your cousin? I had no reason."

Symon grunted. The wind got up but his lank hair didn't blow. 'What reason did your clan ever need to kill a Kirkless?"

As if on cue, the enormous croc let out a low growl.

"This is madness!" protested Fray. "I'm falsely accused!"

"Enough!" declared Symon. "Save it for the trial."

Fray looked like a condemned man who'd just finished his last meal. The adrenalin in his muscles ordered him to flee but his hands were cable-tied. Even if he could swim for it, the croc would rip him to bloody pieces. Tymon Kirkless clapped his huge hand onto the condemned man's shoulder. Then Jem spoke up.

"Hands off our prisoner!" she called, baring the way.

Hanzi smiled nervously at Tymon. The barger was a brute of a man. He looked like he could swat the YPD like a mosquito.

"Shouldn't we just let them take him?" suggested Hanzi.

"No!" said Jem. "Fray is under-age. You just scanned him."

Jem wasn't so sure. Fray could easily pass for an over 16. And he probably had the sort of friends who could hack the clock in the age-chip. Symon Kirkless gave a short pull on the lead and the croc obliged by letting out a roar in Hanzi's direction.

"Are you calling us liars?" he hissed. His hand brushed the shuriken on his belt. "Careful little man. Or you'll be seeing stars."

Jem considered the best course of action. The self-righteous stares of the Kirklesses had the grim look of truth to them.

"Keep talking," said Jem. "How do you know he's over age?"

Symon Kirkless spat sideways into the water.

"Everyone knows Fray. He's the Ferryman's son," he said. "And everyone knows he's nineteen years old if he's a day."

Tymon gave his brother a dark look. Blabbing about Fray's age to the coppers would not play well with Uncle Aeson.

"You... hacked your age-chip?" yelled Hanzi in disgust.

"What do you mean officer?" protested Fray.

"Move," said Tymon, prodding Fray in the ribs.

"Leave it Jem," said Hanzi. But Jem was already moving her hand towards her tazer. Hanzi saw the movement and stepped in front of Jem, drawing his own weapon. As quick as a snake, Symon's metal fist struck out.

Hanzi held his head. The back of his skull burned from the blow.

"Okay! Take him!" Hanzi moaned. "But we're calling this in..."

Symon slowly shook his head and his brother wagged a finger.

"You're coming too now copper," said Tymon. "But your partner stays here. A trial is no place for womenfolk."

Chapter 7: Memorabilia

WITH A NOD OF THE HEAD THAT COULD HAVE BEEN MISTAKEN FOR A
BOW, SHAMI OFFERED THE MASK TO THE FERRYMAN.

If looks were spears, Shami would have harpooned the old
man. The things she'd had to do to retrieve the mask made her
shudder. 'Go to Stormfather island' they'd told her, not mentioning
that the island was crawling with YPD. The islanders worshipped
a mad chief – Badmask they'd called him. It was the madman's
mask she'd had to steal. She'd been lucky to get off that forsaken
rock alive – and twice as lucky to come back without threadneedle.
There was something about that mask. The islanders reckoned it
had some kind of creepy hold on its owner. Shami could believe it.

"That mask has got the mark," she insisted.

The Ferryman took hold of the mask. The skin on his hands
was creased like brown paper. Shami waited as he examined the
symbols on the back of the mask. They looked old enough. The
weight of the thing was right. This mask had to be the one.

"It's real!" she said defensively. "Feel the weight of it."

The Ferryman held the mask up to the glowing lamp. The ancient plastic was solid and heavy, not like the cheap resin they used in the fab machines these days. The old man sucked his yellow teeth. After a long moment he answered. But his eyes gave away the answer and before he spoke.

"Sorry child. It's real. But it's not the one I'm after."

Shami said nothing. She stood there under the glow of the guttering lamp light, her bottom jaw dropping, her head shaking.

Are you blind? It bears the mark!

"There are two marks," the Ferryman said sadly. "Your mask has the first mark all right."

He indicated the PP stamp. Shami knew this symbol of the Pastkeeper's Palace. Every child knew that one. "But it does not have the green wheel. The Greenwheel sigel is a design like this."

"You'll still pay," said Shami.

It was a statement – not a question.

Before Shami could reply they were interrupted by the sound of boots clattering down the wooden stairs. Two figures entered the room. The first wore a robot mask – its emotionless eyes drowned the corridor in a weird red light. The Ferryman's eyes flashed.

"What in the name of Three-Jane do you think you're wearing lad?" he demanded. It was impossible for the robot to look wounded, but its voice made up for it.

"What... the mask?" moaned the first robot.

"Of course the mask!" snapped the old man.

"We got them, just like you said Dadder," put in the second robot. The Ferryman sank back into his chair in desperation.

"I told you to steal them, not WEAR them for all the world to see. You look a right couple of Jillys, the pair of you."

Shami tried not to smirk as the hapless lads removed the masks.

"What are you doing here anyway?" demanded the Ferryman.

"This is men's talk," he added.

"Shami is busy minding MY business lads," hissed the Ferryman.

Shami returned the taller boy's hostile stare. His name was Hal and now that he had his robot mask off, Shami saw that the most noticable thing about him was an unruly mop of bright red curls and bright blue eyes. His brother Atticus seemed to have ignored his father's jibe. He still wore the robot mask.

"Speak up then lads? What is it?" said the Ferryman.

"We've heard that The Wounded Siren has been sunk," said Hal. "They're saying we did it."

"Seven stars," moaned the Ferryman. "Who's saying that?"

"The Kirklesses, dadder," explained the Hal

"Ma says they're all riled up about a killing too. One of their lads was fletched last night."

The Ferryman rose out of his rocking chair to issue commands.

"Double the watch," he told the robot masked boy.

Chapter 8: Alone

JEM STARED AT THE GREY RIPPLES AND WONDERED HOW SHE WAS GOING TO GET OUT OF THIS ONE.

As the Kirklesses' boat rolled away, Jem went over the chain of events that had left her stranded on a one tree island. There had been no point in trying to fight them. They'd taken Hanzi and Fray, commandeering the YPD launch and Fray's gondola in the process.

"The trial is not for womenfolk," the big one had said.

Jem knew that for bargers, 'women's work' meant anything that required an education. So why weren't there any women at the trial? Lawyers crave paperwork like sharks crave blood.

It is the nature of the mind to race and Jem's thoughts skipped back to her own situation as the sun dipped.

The 'island' where the Kirklesses' had left her was little more than a clump of twisted alder trees, clogged with decades of non-degradable plastic. There was a beach of sorts. But it looked like a beggar had thrown a handful of stones into the mud. Unusual noises came from the somewhere in the tangle of alder roots and plastic. The inhabitants of the island were getting active in the dusk. Jem had a terror of rats. Not only because of their disgusting naked tails, but because they carried the threadneedle disease. People were begging the authorities for trapping squads to deal with the creatures. She picked up the largest stone, it was heavy. She was about to throw it at the rat-bush in a preemptive strike when she heard a sound in the still evening air.

Hey!
Over here!

At first she was sure that the boat had failed to spot her. But after about a minute of frantic shouting and waving, she saw the prow twitch and turn in her direction. Gradually the black spot grew larger and the motor's whisper grew to a thrum. Who would be using a diesel motor out here, Jem wondered. Engines had been forbidden years ago by the motor law (a section of the Agreement). But barger waters were not like any other place in London. They had their own law made by Fray's father: the Ferryman. As the boat grew from a black speck to a recognisable vessel, Jem tried to puzzle it out. Fray said he was innocent. But the Kirkless flagship – The *Wounded Siren* – had been sunk.

The ancient boatman thought over Jem's request, rolling an oar nervously through his gnarled hands. The tradition was that

anyone could demand an audience with the Ferryman – the
barger king. Jem knew it from the old stories. But the tradition only
applied if you were a barger. Jem had hung out with one of them
as a girl and in some respects she preferred their way of life. But
eating croc-sticks, wearing a scarf and playing skip-stars with
barger kids when you were supposed to be at school was not the
same as 'belonging' to the community. She'd found that out at a
young age. One of the barger women used to call her 'the myna
bird' implying that she was copying the barger accent.

Tears welled in Jem's eyes as she thought of it. She looked at
the boatman. He had a face like a grape that had withered on the
vine. A face that had never seen moisturising UV block. He was
having none of it.

Jem pleaded with her eyes. It was her only ticket off this rat
hole before sundown.

"I don't need an introduction. Only a ride to the Ferryman's
boat," she said. "I'll even swim the last part so you'll not be
obliged to introduce me." Finally she added, "There's coin too."

The old boatman stopped and the motor revs lowered.

"How much?" he asked through yellow tombstone teeth.

"Twenty swipes," said Jem. The bargers still used the slang 'swipe' for chip coin although the last plastic card had been swiped and charged long before the Climate Upgrade.

There was a loud rustle as something moved in the bushes. Jem looked scared – and it wasn't an act. She took the scarf she'd been waving and drew it around her head in the manner of barger womenfolk. A ray of sunlight suddenly caught Jem's badge, lighting up the unicorn emblem. The barger, whom everyone called 'Old Crow' broke into a toothless smile. Unicorns are lucky, he thought.

Jem stepped gratefully into the boat and stood at the prow.

Looking back at the island, she saw that the rats had come out of their bushes and taken the island back from the invading humans. Rats had their own distinct culture. It was a shame that humans were appropriating it, Jem thought.

Chapter 9: Lock and key

THE GONDOLA BOBBED OBEDIENTLY BEHIND THE KIRKLESSES' BOAT. Like its owner, it had been tied up securely. The green eyes of its idol had been extinguished.

"Detaining a YPD officer against their will is a criminal offence," called Hanzi. There was no reply from outside the wheelhouse. The shouting was serving no purpose and it was getting on Fray's nerves.

"Save your breath officer," he sighed. "Nobody's listening."

Hanzi twisted around and looked through the porthole. Twilight revealed a darkening sky salted with uncountable bright stars. A tall shape loomed up, a vibrant black against the lighter sky behind it. Hanzi recognised the silhouette of the mech that marked the boundary of the Kirkless kingdom. The rusting sentinel hadn't moved in years but it still held a menacing intensity.

Where are these criminals taking us?

Fray bit his lip. They weren't far from the Ferryman's waters. If only he could get a signal out, his father would surround this boat with a flotilla of armed militia. Fray hated the idea of begging for his father's help. However, undoubtably his dadder could make the Kirklesses pay for their treachery. Sadly there was no way to get a message out. Fray's communications gear was back on the gondola. Their boat cruised unhindered through the wide channel. It was headed south towards a line of shapes on the horizon. Hanzi squinted. Before he could work out where they were headed, the door opened to reveal the considerable bulk of Tymon Kirkless.

"Get up!" ordered the voice. Without warning Hanzi was seized by a hand that was bigger than the average oar blade. Both prisoners were man-handled out onto the deck. It was now fully dark but high above him there was familiar yellow glow of oil lamps and the familiar fishy smell from the burning krill oil.

"Hush!" ordered a stern voice. "What did I just tell you?"

"What do you mean Uncle?" moaned Tymon, his thick lips moved something but no coherent words came out.

"Spit it out boy!" yelled the man in the preacher's hat. His face came to life as he willed himself to anger. There was an angry clack as he stomped forward. Hanzi saw that the old barger had a metal blade where his left leg used to be. An expression of fear and bewilderment came over Tymon's face. His uncle unclipped a whip

50

from his belt and wagged it disapprovingly at the big man.

"About secrets..." prompted his brother Symon.

Stung by the blow, Tymon said nothing.

"Secrets are ours for keeping," said Symon, who could not bear to see his big brother tormented like this.

"Sorry uncle Aeson!" sobbed Tymon. "I forgot!"

Aeson's cold eyes narrowed and flashed with rage.

Chapter 10: The Ferryman

JEM'S EYES WIDENED AS THEY APPROACHED THE TOWERING MECH.

The angle made it impossible for Jem to see the stunned look on the guard's face. But there was no argument. The boatman dropped a coin into the box on the mech's knee and swiped the ceremonial card. Bargers still swiped for luck even though cards were useless since the cloud had died.

Crow flicked a switch and turned on the running lights. To the rest of London, the bargers were a enigma. They claimed to be too poor to send their male children to school, yet they would happily burn precious electricity on things like ornamental lights for a gondola. Jem saw the eyes of the idol on the back of their boat light up. Chains of expensive lights hung around the their craft, casting a gaudy green aura.

Jem yawned and rubbed her eyes. They'd reached their destination – a galley that looked like it had sailed out of the pages of history. The Ferryman's boat had what looked like Little Red Riding Hood as a figure head. She was cloaked inglimmering neon. If I were a wolf, I'd be scared – Jem thought. But there weren't any wolves left. The last wolf had died thirty years ago.

Jem threw a rope to a couple of surly looking deckhands who stood idling with their grimy hands in their pockets. The nearest youth deliberately failed to catch Crow's rope and it fell back into the black water. Jem called over to him.

Jem wasn't satisfied with this answer but she kept the frustration out of her voice.

"Why not? Is it because I'm a girl? Or because I'm YPD?"

The tone was light, like that of two friends sharing a joke.

"Take your pick," came the reply. "Either one will do."

There was a peel of laughter from the crew. The old boatman looked at Jem and spat into the water with an 'I told you so' expression on his weather-worn face. But Jem wasn't giving up that easily.

"I have news of Fray, the Ferryman's son," called Jem, adopting a serious tone to signal that the time for joking was over. But it didn't seem to make any difference.

A tall woman joined the group. Despite her advancing years she held herself straight and her voice still held considerable power.

"I'll do more than shame you. Your half brother is missing. Kidnapped by Aeson Kirkless and his crew. What do you want? A rope for him?"

The guard shook his head and sighed.

"Shut up and let this girl on board. Your father will hear what she's got to say."

Jem followed the sulky youth below deck, through a series of hatches and ladders, until they finally reached a sturdy oak door. When the boy knocked, it swung open on silent hinges. Jem edged forward to find herself standing in front of an old man sitting in a carved oak rocking chair. A masked guard stood behind in the shadows.

Jem said her piece. The tale was long in the telling – how she had caught Fray stealing electricity from the fence. How they'd seen the Kirkless boat sinking. The quarrel that led to the abduction of her partner Hanzi and Fray by the Kirkless security guards. As she finished the tale, the Ferryman tapped out his pipe. Coils of smoke filled the cabin. The old man's blue eyes were sad.

"My partner Hanzi is in danger," said Jem. "I guess I should have called it in to YPD headquarters."

The robotic red eyes glared at Jem.

"Don't shoot the messenger!" said Jem. Her tone was defensive. She tried to out glare the robot but it had lights instead of eyes.

"Atticus!" growled the Ferryman. "Here's me telling Jem she's done the right thing to come to me with this. And you're stepping up to the girl with your hands raised. You're acting like a Kirkless."

Admonished, the robot deactivated its red eyes and sulked.

"She's got more to tell us, I'll warrant," added the Ferryman.

"Not much," said Jem. "Only we need to find the real sinker. That'll get your son off the hook. They'll have to release my partner Hanzi too."

The Ferryman tapped out his pipe on the side of the chair.

"I have someone who works for me – who'll help you sort this. The pair of you will get on famously. Go and fetch her lad."

The robot slunk of obediently. It wasn't long before the door swung silently open.

57

Shami regarded her foe with a blend of interest and disgust. Jem's jaw seemed to be on wires. She just gaped at Shami.

"Come on ladies, what's the problem?"

The Ferryman turned towards Shami, inviting her to speak. There was no accusation in the look.

"Mallard hunted down my friends," said Shami matter-of-factly. "Some of them are still rotting in the Tower because of her."

Jem turned her attention to the Ferryman, her big eyes shining like twin head lamps through the smoky darkness.

"Father Thames?" hissed Jem. "It's a dead organization – there's only her and my mother left by the look of it."

Shami shook her head defiantly.

"Father Thames was never an organisation," she said.

Jem let out a mocking laugh and turned to the Ferryman, like a lawyer addressing a jury.

"Father Thames are insane," she said slowly.

Shami shook her head adamantly.

"Father Thames was always an alliance of like minds."

But the old man fell silent for a moment, lost in his thoughts. Finally he turned and looked pointedly at the door to the room with the masks. Jem saw only a half open wooden door, but it lit the fuse of her curiosity. The Ferryman opened his mouth as if he was about to speak but something held him back.

"The truth about what?" repeated Jem. The question was urgent but there was no anger in it. Instinctively, she knew she'd taken him to the point of a revelation. A silence now might have drawn the secret out of him. But in her haste, she repeated the question.

"First to the business in hand. My son Frey is not a bad lad. He's done a few wild things since his mother passed – but he's not a killer, or a sinker. Find out who sunk the Kirklesses' boat..."

The Ferryman's words trailed off and all eyes fell on the door to the mask room.

"Find the sinker. Then I'll let you in on the secret."

Shami had stood silent through all of this.

"I don't work with YPD," she said in a low voice.

The Ferryman nodded.

"You'll make an exception, think of it as a favour to my family."

Thoughts swam around Jem's mind in shoals. Father Thames was working with the bargers? What was hidden behind the Ferryman's locked door? Ask any YPD what you'd find in a barger's cabin and they'd tell you it was contraband or smuggled weapons. But the Ferryman was different. He was seeking the truth. Whatever the revelation was – Jem would have to earn the information by solving the mystery of the sinking. Shami scowled at Jem.

"I'm not working with her. I'd rather share a boat with a serpent."

Jem said nothing but the look in her eyes screamed: "Likewise!"

"Where do we start looking?" she asked.

"Atticus will take you over to the Kirkless waters," said the Ferryman, nodding to one of the figures in the robot masks.

"Shall I go with them father?" asked the second robot.

"No Hal. We don't want to start World War IV," said the Ferryman.

Shami glared at Jem. Jem glared back. The Ferryman ignored the antagonism between the two girls. He unlocked a cabinet, slid open a wooden drawer, produced a small leather bag and handed it to Jem.

This is for you.

What is it?

It's from your mother.

61

Chapter 11: Colony

Hanzi stared at the wall, stared at the bars, stared at the floor.

The mission was drifting out of control. After the meeting with Uncle Aeson, The Kirkless boys had locked him up with Fray. As far as he could see, he was in some kind of old cargo container from the trading age. The walls were solid – double skinned steel – too thick for a signal to get through. Outside, a storm was brewing.

"I've been thinking," said Hanzi. "If you want me to speak for you at the trial… then I'm afraid it's a no."

Fray looked at Hanzi. His face expressionless, his body motionless.

"You've broken the law," explained Hanzi. "Hacking an age chip is a serious offence under section 23 of the YPD code. I'm afraid it's impossible for me to appear in your defence."

"Combat?" repeated Hanzi, trying to retain control of his voice. At that moment someone hit the outside of the metal container with a heavy object, making it ring like a lighthouse bell. Hanzi's hopes turned to rescue until he heard the slow voice of Tymon.

"Sun's rising. Time to pay for your crimes," it called.

"What crimes?" protested Fray. "I'm innocent."

Tymon's laughter was cold and metallic. There was a scraping noise of cold metal sliding on rusted tracks as Tymon slid back a vent panel. Hanzi peered out of the opening. The river was dirty steel, the sky a spectral pre-dawn grey.

Chapter 12: Giant

JEM STUDIED THE YOUTH IN THE ROBOT MASK.

"Don't you ever take that mask off?" asked Jem.

"Negative!" chimed a metallic voice. The red eyes were creepy – but talking to Atticus was better than trying to make conversation with the brooding presence of Shami, who was trying on a mask of her own. It was a white tribal horror, borrowed from the Ferryman's collection. Jem knew Shami hated her – blaming the YPD for the death of the Father Thames leadership. She wondered what kind of secret could be big enough to link Shami and the Ferryman? Their boat glided towards another abandoned mech. Barger waters were dotted with them. Jem noted a strong resemblance between Atticus's mask and the face of the rusting giant. That was so weird.

As the boat passed under the shadow of the mech, Jem felt a vibration coming from the bag in her pocket. She pulled it out. Jem's eyes were drawn to a blue glow that was coming through the material.

"What's in the bag Mallard?" asked Shami, who had suddenly appeared at Jem's shoulder. Jem recoiled from Shami's hideous mask. At first she'd thought it was African, but now she recognised the mask as Japanese. Some kind of fox character perhaps?

"Looks like something's activated," said Atticus.

Before Jem could answer, all hell broke loose. Waves rocked the boat violently and it rolled and pitched as if seized by a giant's hand. Jem's shouts were lost in the spray and the wind.

"Who'd plant mines here?" Jem moaned. It was a stupid question so Shami didn't answer. Power jackers, mercs, privateers, one of the many barger clans out for revenge. In Shami's world, violence was a certainty, like heavy weather. It didn't need a reason.

"This is a present from the Kirklesses," announced Atticus.

He was working quickly, patching the gash in the hull with an ancient can of auto-weld.

"Nice," said Jem. "It's 7am and someone is trying to kill us."

"No…" said Atticus, inspecting the welding job.

"I was thinking," began Jem. "Who would benefit from sinking the Kirklesses' boat? Killing that kid?"

Jem looked at Shami, there was no accusation in the look but maybe just a faint hint of suspicion. "Someone who wants to start a war between you and the Kirklesses?" she added.

"Not START a war," corrected Atticus. "The war between the Ferrymen family and clan Kirkless started long ago."

"Who's the head of their clan?" asked Jem.

"Officially, it's old Dadder Kirkless. He was as mean as a viper in his youth. But his brother Aeson is the one to fear now."

Chapter 13: High water

AESON KIRKLESS STEPPED ONTO THE PLATFORM LIKE THE RINGMASTER AT A NIGHTMARE CIRCUS. He pulled his hat down, coughed and raised a skinny hand with a sweep. With a rattle of tappets the crane clattered into life. The diesel engine was given the death sentence back in 2030, condemned for its micro pollutants that caused cancer. But it was a suspended sentence. Plenty of engines had been 'refabed' after the Climate Upgrade failed. Diesel motors can run on any hydrocarbon: krill oil, kerosene or paraffin. It was a wonder how the oil companies kept that quiet for so long. Mushrooms of black smoke putted from the crane's twin exhaust pipes, hovering above the water like unquiet ghosts.

Hanzi and Fray clung to the bars as the container swung gently on its iron chain. It was a bit like being inside an ancient 'grabber' game. In a cloud of smoke they were lowered down towards the unforgiving water. Hanzi had always feared drowning – it was the most common cause of death for YPD officers. As the container tracked slowly out towards the centre of the arena, Hanzi thought he saw dark shapes moving under the surface.

Hanzi's face turned the same greenish white shade you see on a croc's underbelly. How much did the bargers know? Deciding that deflection was the best defence, he turned to his fellow prisoner.

"Look Fray," he said. "There's no point in both of us dying. Confess to the sinking and I promise that I'll fight to clear your name – posthumously."

Fray shot Hanzi a look and was about to speak but the cage rocked and lurched. Hanzi's hand went to the buckle of his belt. Inside the buckle was a transmission device. Hanzi picked his moment and slid the switch to the 'transmit' position. Fray didn't notice. Not being noticed came easily to Hanzi. The transmitter in his belt was sending out a signal. But would his bosses feel that he was an asset worth saving? Hanzi reflected on his mission.

His orders had been to start a war between the two most important barger clans: the Ferrymen and the Kirklesses. The clan war would provide a pretext for a take over of barger territory. Unusually, both police forces – the APD and Hanzi's own YPD – were working together to start the war. Exactly why the two police forces wanted control of barger waters was above Hanzi's pay grade. There was nothing of interest in the area, except the Pastkeeper's Palace. But that was sealed up and only opened once every seven years.

Weirder still was the choice of Jem Mallard as his partner. She had no idea about the mission's true objectives – so it was a risk to have her so close to the operation. Hanzi knew all about Jem Mallard – she was under surveillance by both forces because of her links to terrorists. Her mother was the founder of Father Thames organisation.

Hanzi knew that his bosses were playing a slow and intricate game. Father Thames were said to be working with the bargers. Perhaps they thought Jem Mallard might lead the YPD to her terrorist mother? Mallard had certainly been taken in by Hanzi's spoilt brat act. He'd given her a character that confirmed her preconceptions: the self-important kid.

When Hanzi heard his mission's objectives he'd laughed. Bargers were famous for feuding. Getting them fighting would be easy. And so it had proved. One of his contacts had provided him with Fray's fletch. He'd fed Mallard a story about looking to buy a second hand tazor battery from a barger, and he'd slipped away for the night. Then he'd planted the device on the Wounded Siren and taken the shot. The

Kirkless kid went down with Fray's fletch in his chest. The next day, the mission seemed to be running on rails. Even the bomb had gone off according to plan. But then they'd run into Kirklesses security. At first Hanzi had thought it was a stroke of luck. If Tymon and Symon had been allowed to drag Fray off to the trial, the mission would have been complete. Fray would have been murdered as payback for the dead Kirkless boy. The Ferryman's people would take revenge, starting a barger clan war. But Jem Mallard hadn't wanted to let the Kirklesses take Fray. These thoughts were interrupted by a wild shout from outside the cage. Tymon smiled in triumph, swinging the container downwards with a jarring clank as the rusted chain paid out.

Chapter 14: Seagull

SHAMI GLARED AT THE PROPELLER, AS IF BY STARING AT IT SHE COULD WILL THE BOAT TO MOVE FASTER OVER THE CHOPPY WATER.

"We need more speed," yelled Shami, yelling to make herself heard over the whirr of the aircraft style propeller. "Does this boat have any mods?"

Atticus's robot eyes stared blankly back at her.

"Come on!" said Shami. "Stop holding out. It must have some sort of modifications. Barger boats always have tricks."

Shami looked at Atticus with a sullen exasperation on her face.

"I hate to admit it," said Jem. "But she's right. If you want to save your brother and that idiot partner of mine, we need speed." The masked barger cut the propeller and the engine died. Then he slid a gloved hand under the forward rail and flipped a hidden switch. A panel appeared, bristling with backlit controls. Shami smiled. The bargers love a bit of theatre. They'd even drawn a red explosion under the button marked: 'Fire!'

Shami spotted a button with a child's drawing taped under it.

But before Shami could hit the boost button, Jem blocked her hand. She pointed at a green joystick with an unusual label.

"Seagull?" said Jem incredulously. Don't tell me you've weaponised seagulls?"

Atticus caught the critical tone in Jem's voice.

"There's no weapons," he said reassuringly. "Just an old camera."

Jem looked relieved. There was something supremely arrogant about humanity – the sort of cold thinking that tied explosives onto dolphins and bred genetically modified rats with gills.

Atticus flicked a switch and a matt green metal grill slid back to uncover a large wooden cage. A big seagull hopped out onto the wooden deck. It was wearing a leather collar, the sort of thing that a hunting hawk might wear. It didn't look comfortable.

"Can it fly with that thing on?" asked Shami.

"Sure she can. They're strong birds," said Atticus defensively.

"What button do I press to launch?" asked Jem, eyeing the control panel. The robot's mask tilted sideways in disbelief.

"What button to launch the seagull???!!" scoffed Shami.

Jem folded her arms defensively and turned to Atticus.

"You're the one with the button marked 'seagull' on your panel," said Jem in an injured tone. "What does the joystick do?"

"Taking a wild guess, I'd say it moves the camera," said Shami.

"So how do we launch?" asked Jem.

Atticus made shooing gestures and the bird took off.

"Fly my beauty!" he said in a robotic voice.

The gull let out a wail and took off, wheeling high into the sky.

"Haven't you heard of drones?" asked Shami.

"Sure," said Atticus. "But drones can't fly all day on fish scraps."

"What now?" asked Jem, craning up at the disappearing bird.

"When she gets high," said Atticus. "We take a picture."

"You mean you can beam the images back here and display them on a screen?" asked Jem, whistling appreciatively.

"Nope," said Atticus.

"So how DO we view the picture?" demanded Jem.

"We wait for her to fly back," explained the amused barger.

"Could be a long wait," said Jem straining her eyes. The seagull was now no more than a white dot against the grey dawn sky.

"No sweat," said Atticus. "This'll bring her back."
He fished around in a cubby hole and pulled out a leather bag. The pungent reek of rotting fish filled the still air.

"Seagull snacks?" asked Jem. "If it works, I'm not knocking it."

"Just take the picture," said Shami. "We're wasting time."
It didn't take long. Ten minutes later the seagull was back on the boat spearing snacks from the leather bag as Atticus retrieved a small square of paper from the harness on the gull's neck.

"The picture is blank," said Jem in disappointment. "Your camera must be broken."

"I told you this was a waste of time," hissed Shami.

"Hold on," said Atticus. "It's called an instax. It'll appear before your eyes like magic."

Chapter 15: The trial

As far as Fray could make out, two thirds of the barger clans were at the trial – with the exception of clans allied to the Ferryman or any of Fray's family. The array of boats belonged to clans loyal to the Kirklesses. The Morrows were there, tall men with rising sun decals on their prows. The Creeks had come too – with grinning skulls on the fans of their airboats. Then Fray spotted a familiar sight: was that Old Crow's gondola with its distinctive prow? Crow was a regular sight at the Ferryman's wharf. He was no friend of the Kirklesses. Then Fray spotted his own gondola – tied to a pontoon bridge. One of the Kirkless boys would claim it for his own when this was over. Big Tymon was working the crane, whilst Symon was down at the waterside, with that dumb croc of his on a leash. It wasn't long before the crowd got what they'd come for. The crane released the cage and the cable screamed out from the pulley. Fray braced himself for impact as the cage smashed into the water with a smack. Symon Kirkless shouted across from the platform.

The container was flooding fast. Fray felt an arm on his right shoulder. It was Hanzi. The YPD was trying to tell him something but before he could make out what was being said, there was a sudden lurch. The crane's ancient engine started and the cage was hauled up out of the water again.

"Which of you killed our kin?" demanded Aeson Kirkless, shaking his boney fist. Cold water gushed into the cage. Hanzi was up to his neck in it. Fray shouted desperate protests.

A low rumble of ascent passed through the crowd. Fray pleaded that it WAS his fletch but it had gone missing a few days before. He was in the area BEFORE the sinking but on his way to the fence. He had no reason to want a Kirkless dead. None of these arguments hit the mark. When he ran out of things to say Aeson's shark grey eyes were still on him.

Chapter 16: Dawning

TIME WAS RUNNING FAST, LIKE A TIDE ON THE TURN. The picture from the seagull-cam showed a flotilla of small boats crowed around a floating platform. Atticus immediately recognised boats belonging to the Kirklesses and their crew. Jem didn't know what they were up to. But what decent thing could involve a crane, a cage and crocodiles?

"That's my brother's boat," said Atticus, realisation dawning as he spoke the words. Jem sensed his fear, even though the speech synthesiser in the robot mask sucked the emotion from his voice.

"It's Fray's gondola," gasped Jem. "Take us in."

"There'll be guards so act normally," suggested the barger.

Shami eased the throttle forward and the motor responded. The boat rose up on its hydrofoil, picking up speed.

Jem gripped the polished wooden rail as they crested over the grey chop. One hand for the ship, and one for yourself – just like her father had taught her. Atticus pulled out a harpoon gun. After checking the weapon he turned back to Jem, his robot eyes glowing like embers.

"How comforting!" said Shami in a mocking voice. "A wolf girl, a robot boy and a lone YPD against clan Kirkless and all their henchmen. There must be at least fifty cold blooded killers out there. Not including the crocodiles."

"Who do we target?" asked Jem through gritted teeth.

"Anyone except the hostages," said Atticus practically. "But first we've got to get past the guards."

Without another word Shami grabbed Jem's arms and wrenched them behind her back. Jem squirmed and wriggled, spitting insults. The girl in the Japanese mask let out a wicked laugh.

"Captive?" protested Jem. She struggled to wrench her arms free but failed. Shami's thin arms had a surprising strength.

"Play along with me Mallard," hissed Shami under her breath. "I'm going to make this look authentic for the Kirklesses."

Chapter 17: Defenders

THE WATCHERS HEARD THE AIR BOAT BEFORE THEY SAW IT. Atticus waved enthusiastically to the two figures on the pontoon guarding the entrance to the floating 'court'. Shami yanked at the rope around Jem's neck causing her to choke. She's enjoying making it authentic – thought Jem. Instinctively, she tore at the rope around her neck.

"Morning kinsfolk!" called Atticus.

One of the guards bit down on a plug of tobacco. Jem winced. These guard looked like he'd walked out of a propaganda poster. All that was missing was the shuriken. As if on cue, he produced one of the famous barger throwing stars from his belt.

"What's your business?" demanded the smaller guard.

"Folks call us The Masked Defenders," said Atticus pointing a gloved finger to indicate his masked face.

"The Masked Defenders are always ready," said Atticus.

The big guard had cow eyes to go with his bull neck. His friend had a bald head that looked like a boiled egg that had been left in the pan for too long. The guards studied the newcomers.

"Get those masks off!" demanded the bull. "No one comes in unless we see their faces."

"I'd love to oblige friend," said Shami coolly. "But if we took our masks off, we wouldn't be The Masked Defenders anymore."

The guard spat out a plug of half-chewed tobacco – a disgusting habit straight out of the henchmen's handbook, thought Jem. The baccy hit the croc behind its collar. The beast submerged itself.

"Aeson will have something to say about this," said Atticus.

"Aeson?" muttered the guard. "Are you working for Aeson?"

"It was Aeson who set up The Masked Defenders. Extra security for today," offered Atticus. "So are you letting us pass?"

"Out of the boat!" said the guard.

Then three things happened at once. Shami put the boat into gear, punched the throttle and gave Jem a hard push in the back.

81

The boat surged forwards, gunning at the barrier at full speed. The hapless Kirkless guards scrambled to cling onto their jetty as a great wave from the boat washed over them.

The cold water drew a gasp from Jem. What in Fill's name was Shami playing at?

Struggling for breath, Jem swam towards the wooden platform in the middle of the ring of boats. She saw the cage being lowered into the water and heard loud shouts from inside. So she changed direction and struck out for the container. Water flooded in through the bars. The rusty iron chain squealed under the weight. After what seemed like an age, the crane drew the container up until it was a few feet above the surface. Water spurted out through bad welds in the floor. Jem reached for the bars and clung on as the cage rose. Then she saw the croc coming at her – like a dragon after an unhorsed knight – its cruel jaws gaping. Jem clambered onto the jetty and drew the tazor from her belt. Electricity and water don't mix, she thought. She was soaking wet. But what other options did she have?

The tazor crackled. The water hissed as sparks skipped along the croc's snout. It rocked back momentarily and sank down into the surface. Then it came at her again. Jem retreated and fired a second shot. An arc of blue sparks flicked over the water.

"Good shot!" said a voice. "Where's the rest of the evacuation team?"

Jem was puzzled. Hanzi didn't seem surprised to see her.

The croc came back to try for another bite. Jem blasted it again.

"You won't stop a croc with a tazor on stun," advised Hanzi matter-of-factly. "That's just a waste of good sparks."

Jem fried him with one of her full-power glares.

"There's still enough juice left to weld your mouth shut," she hissed. "Fine thanks I get for coming out to rescue you."

"You might want to get a move on. Those crocs can jump six metres at feeding time," said Fray, adding "What's the plan?" as he leaned towards her through the bars.

Jem shrugged. "The plan was to get you out," she replied sheepishly. But I seem to have forgotten my lock picking kit."

"Tymon has the key," said Fray.

"Is that Tymon on the platform?" asked Jem. She nodded towards the ranting figure in the preacher's hat. He was stomping his bladed leg on the deck and shaking a skeletal fist.

"Nope," sighed Hanzi. "That's Uncle Aeson. "Tymon is the fat gangster type working the crane that's holding us up."

Jem looked up at the crane. The chain suddenly started to squeal like a pig in a slaughterhouse.

The presence of the newcomer had not gone unnoticed around the ring. The crowd started to point and roar insults.

Aeson Kirkless turned slowly to address Jem.

"Don't interfere girl," he ordered.

84

The reaction from the crowd was mixed. They'd come for a trial by combat, not a drowning. Aeson seemed to hesitate.

"But uncle," called Tymon from the crane. "These crocs are hungry. We didn't feed them breakfast, on account of the trial."

Ignoring the murmurs of protest from the crowd Aeson Kirkless signalled to the crane. Tymon let out a cry of triumph. A flick of the lever sent the chain playing out. Jem's screams were lost as the container hit the water. It rocked and creaked for a long moment. Then finally it began to sink below the oily surface.

Freezing water poured through the bars. Jem sucked in one long final breath – and they were under. Inside the cage, Fray and Hanzi wrenched at the bars as it sank, stopping with a jerk as it reached the end of the chain. Jem felt the pressure of the water on her chest and ears. A green flare of fluorescence pierced the darkness. Hanzi had some kind of emergency lights in his boots. Through the clear water, she saw a line of bubbles leaking from Fray's mouth as he pulled at the bars. There was a look of grim determination in the barger's eyes – but Jem knew it was useless. As a child she'd had played the 'hold your breath' game with all the other kids. After two minutes, everyone tapped out.

Jem reeled. Two white dots were approaching. Gradually, the twin dots resolved into headlights of a diver propulsion vehicle.

Pulling the DPV up by the cage, Atticus produced a pair of scuba masks. Jem took a gulp of air and passed the mask through the cage bars to Fray. For a moment, the bulky mask snagged on the metal and then it was through and Fray was breathing. Working with practiced assurance, Atticus ripped the welding can open and worked on the lock as Hanzi turned away from the light, gulping down air greedily. At last the lock gave in and the door of the cage swung open.

Hanzi and Fray swam through the opening. The diver propulsion unit was little more than a motor mounted on a torpedo shaped frame. They began to move forwards. It was faster than swimming but the DPVs were designed to move one or two divers – not three.

At that moment, a monster loomed towards them out of the murky water. The beast's mouth was horribly wide. Wide enough to swallow a diver. Its tail was fat with crenelated scales, like the top of a castle wall. It gave the impression of a monstrous dragon that had grown fat by eating who knows what. Once a croc gets that big, it rules its territory by eating its family first, Jem remembered. But something else from the lesson stuck in her mind.

"Crocodile's don't bite underwater," was what the croc farmer had told her. "They don't like to bite underwater. They like to rise to the surface to take their prey."

Jem fought to keep that in mind as the monster glided silently past, eying her with a cold glare.

The DPV pulled Jem and Fray slowly through the channel – weighed down by the weight of the passengesr. A few metres above her, Jem could make out the hulls of a line of boats as she passed under them. The progress was painful. The DPV motor whirred bravely but it seemed to be getting slower and slower. In a panic, Jem realised that she was rising to the surface – where the Kirkless's and more crocs were waiting. Jem cautiously stuck her head out of the water, coming up next to Atticus.

"There they are!" cried Symon Kirkless.

"What you waiting for? Shoot em boy!" cried Aeson.

Harpoon darts hit the water with a hiss. There was a dull thud as something metallic connected with the DVP. Jem heard a cry coming from over her left shoulder. A wave hit her full in the face. She spun towards the sound spluttering out a mouthful of river.

Jem accepted Shami's hand without hesitation. The masked girl helped her up into the gondola. Arrows peppered into the idol's face, giving it the look of a porcupine. Gasping for breath. Jem helped to pull Fray and Atticus up into the craft. Hanzi was last, Shami reached towards his outstretched hand but then pulled away.

Jem stared open mouthed with disbelief as the gondola turned away. A steel rain of arrows fell into the water behind them.

"Turn us around," screamed Jem at Fray, her eyes wild.

"It's too late for that," he said flatly. "Here come the Kirklesses."

He pointed at a spot on the horizon where a red shape was heading towards them. The boat was already gaining on them. Fray took the helm and unlocked the boost control, hesitating over the switches. A few seconds later the boat lurched forward.

By now, Jem could make out a couple of figures in the pursuit boat. One of them was the skinny one who'd been standing with the creepy preacher. Jem saw that somehow, Shami had managed to hang on to the fox mask that the Ferryman had given her. She pulled the mask over her face as the boat crashed through a wave, drenching them all with freezing white foam. Jem turned to look back at the figure of her partner Hanzi, now a receding dot in the expanse of grey water.

Whoops of triumph went up from the pursuers as one of the Kirkless boats peeled off and grabbed the unfortunate YPD. Jem contemplated the scene in shocked horror.

"The Kirklesses will kill him," she sighed.

"Don't you know a rat when you smell one?" replied Shami.

Before Jem could answer, Atticus broke the spell.

"They've got a jetboat," he said. "We can't outrun them."

Jem turned her head from the pursing Kirklesses and peered into the misty distance. She could just make out the silhouette of the ancient mech they'd passed on the way out.

"Fray!" called Jem, shouting over the noise of the motor and the wind. "Is that the boundary of Kirkless waters over there?"

Fray nodded. "But it doesn't mean anything. They'll just chase us over the boundary and run us down," he added.

Chapter 18: Faster

SYMON KIRKLESS WHISTLED TUNELESSLY AS HE EYED THE ESCAPING
BOAT. A look of disgust from his uncle stopped him dead.

"FASTER!" demanded Aeson, leaning out in the direction of
the prey. To please his tyrant uncle Symon leaned out towards the
fleeing boat, living every bump and engine rev. The boat's driver,
Thaddeus was more sanguine about it.

"Don't worry Uncle Aeson," said Thaddeus. "There ain't a boat
on the river that can outrun The Impeacher."

Thaddeus patted the wheel of his beloved vessel.
Aeson Kirkless made no reply. His cold preacher's eyes studied the
distance between their boat and the enemy.

Jem looked back at the Kirklesses across the expanse of slate grey
water. She knew she was looking at a fast boat. The Impeacher was
sleek and shark like, its narrow hull leaving surprisingly little wake.
With its twin engines it could outrun even the YPD's fastest craft.

The gap between the two boats narrowed. Atticus weaved a course towards the mech. Now they were just twenty metres away from the rusting giant.

"Cut the engine," said Jem flatly.

"We can't surrender!," said Atticus. "Does not compute."

"Who said anything about surrendering," asked Jem. "Get us in close, on the far side of that mech."

Jem ignored her and squeezed the trigger. The harpoon spat from the gun. Its barb crashed into the old armour and held.

"Follow me!" cried Jem, testing the rope before her swing.

"Abandoning ship?" asked Shami, the mask tipping up on her face as she sneered the rebuke. Jem ignored her and turned to Frey.

"Can you make it look like we're still on our boat?" she asked. "Jam the throttle, tie the steering and send the gondola off?"

Frey gazed back over his shoulder as he contemplated the plan. Atticus exchanged a look with his brother.

"Get going. I'll take care of it," said Frey.

Minutes later, they'd all swung across to the mech and were clinging to a ladder that ran up one of its steel legs.

"What next Mallard?" said Shami.

"The hatch is rusted shut," moaned Jem.

"Never send a human to do a robot's work," roared Atticus. The motors on his powered armour gloves let out a steady whirring as his fingers tightened around the handle. Squeaking in pain, the ancient hatchway gave way with a metallic sigh.

The ladder inside the mech was old but intact. Jem could hear the sound of her own breath as she hauled herself up the steel rungs. It felt good to be out of the wind. As she drew the leather bag out of her pocket, she breathed a sigh of relief and held it up.

"Outstanding!" said Fray, sweeping his hand down the complex array of controls and flicking switches randomly.

"Ignition... ignition..." Atticus mumbled, searching the panel.

"Over there," said Jem, pointing to a sensor. It glowed with the same faint blue light as her key. Fray snatched the key from Jem's hand and touched the sensor.

Emergency lights flooded the space with halogen brightness. Disappointingly, the inside of the mech was the same ogre-green colour as its outside.

Everything about the giant machine was slug-ugly, thought Jem. But the mech had not been built to be admired.

"I'm freezing," said Fray. "You three must have thick skins."

"Wait!" said Atticus. "We don't want to activate anything. We're supposed to be hiding remember?"

"Sorry," said Fray. "But I can't help it if I've got bad circulation."

Jem stifled a laugh.

"Cold blood more like," said Atticus.

Jem looked into the robot's eyes. Under the mask he might have been smiling.

"Quiet!" snapped Shami, "What's that noise?"

Jem looked over her shoulder. There was little enough space for the four of them squeezed into the cramped cabin. Jem stood and listened. Slowly, the sound resolved into something she could recognise: the familiar beat of an outboard.

"It's a motor," moaned Jem.

"The Kirklesses," sighed Shami.

They heard the sound of a boat mooring alongside their mech.

"They'll try to board us," said Atticus. "What do we do now?"

Peering out of the cabin window was no good. The passing

years had turned the clear plexiglass cloudy.

There was a grim inevitability about the whole thing. The Kirklesses were cunning – not as simplistic as they looked. Instead of shooting off in pursuit of the decoy gondola, they'd doubled back. The mech's armour was miliary grade and hard to cut through, but now the defenders were bottled up inside like rats in a steel pipe. There was no way out.

"Anyone got any bright ideas?" asked Jem, checking the battery pack on her tazor.

"They can't get in any time soon," said Atticus. "This thing was built to withstand attackers."

Frey looked worried.

"Mallard – get back there and get it sorted!" ordered Shami.

'Why me?" asked Jem.

"You're the closest," hissed the girl in the mask. "Move it! I'm right behind you."

Jem crawled back down the metal tunnel. The red emergency lighting lent the pale green walls a yellow brown hue like the colour of sick Jem found herself thinking. She wondered what in seven seas she'd got herself into this time. For all she knew, a hunting party of armed Kirklesses were coming towards her down the tunnel. Unless they'd sent in croc or two to do a their hunting for them.

"Wait!" called Shami, putting a finger over the lips of her mask and pointing a lean arm towards the end of the corridor. The tunnel shook with the force of repeated blows. Then the banging stopped abruptly.

"Told you I'd sealed that hatch," said Jem.

There was something about Shami that brought out her childish side. The banging noise started up again. Clan Kirkless were hard at work on the door.

"What now?" asked Jem. But Shami wasn't listening. Pulling her mask up she stood staring at a panel on the right-hand wall. She didn't notice the intensity in Shami's gaze. This was no time for wall-gazing. But the wisecrack died on Jem's lips.

The logo was a banded globe divided into two. In one segment was a mechanical cog like the wheel in some ancient engine. The letters G.W. stood out in a confident font.

"What does G.W. stand for?" asked Jem.

"Get walking!" said Shami, hustling her forwards.

A few metres later they turned a corner and found the ladder that led to the entrance. Muffled shouts came from the outside. As she climbed, Jem thought about the G.W. logo and experienced a nagging feeling. Her subconscious was whispering that she'd seen that logo before. The whisper persisted. Jem struggled to will the lost word into her conscious mind. But when a word is on the tip of your tongue, effort of thought does no good. You might as well will the wind to stop blowing. Exasperated, Jem turned her attention back to the door. The banging had stopped but whisps of white smoke were rising slowly from the door.

"Can they burn through the lock?" asked Jem. Shami lowered her mask with one hand and raised the tazor with the other.

Jem shook with rage. "What in Fill's name do you think you're doing mother?"

"Do I need a reason to visit my darling daughter," asked River.

The years had been kind but the thin spider's web of fine lines still marked her cheek – remnants of the threadneedle disease.

"Shami dearest," said River. "Be a love and make room."

Shami stepped back to make room for River. Jem peered through the smoking door and saw another familiar face waiting for her.

"Old Crow!" she gasped, looking at the wizened face of the boatman – standing bent-backed like Charon in the mist. "I thought I saw his boat at the trial. Is Crow working for...?"

"Me," interrupted River. "He's got a face like old Father Thames himself. But there's absolutely no the time for catch ups. Your Kirkless friends and their reptiles are lurking nearby."

Jem glowered petulantly, like a child who'd just been asked to leave a sweet shop and did not want to comply. The 'ready' light on her tazor was still blinking.

"Why did you burn through the hatch?" demanded Jem.

"I tried a polite knock but there was no answer," smiled River.

"Why...?" gasped Jem, a single hot tear running down her cheek.

"What do you mean – why?" asked River slowly. "If you're going to risk your life wasting time with silly questions, you may as well use fully formed sentences."

River smiled. "It's not all about you dear...." But the words petered out. "Although in a way, it IS always all about you Jem," she laughed. Shami suppressed a sigh. Jem glared at both of them. River ignored Shami and spoke with a calm purpose, proceeding like a lawyer at a trial.

"Last time we met I asked you to join Father Thames," began River.

"Sorry mother," said Jem flatly. I'm not really a joiner."

River sighed. "I know you're not Jemima," she replied. "But you can't resist a mystery."

"What mystery?" demanded Jem.

"Which mystery shall we tackle first?" laughed River. "Big, bigger or biggest?"

"Let's start small," said Jem, ever the contrarian.

"I honestly have no idea. Enlighten me mother," sighed Jem. Jem already knew what her mother was going to say. It was predictable as sunrise. Jem felt queasy, as she did whenever she saw the storm clouds brewing in her mother's fragile mind.

Tears welled up and Jem fought them, her fingernails biting into her clenched fist. Her mother was a monomaniac when it came to her father. She viewed the APD as an occupying power and DCI Mallard as a leading collaborator with the forces of evil.

"How can dad be behind this?" Jem scoffed. "He's a sick man. The only reason I'm here is to pay for his meds."

River took the mask from Shami and held it up to her face. "I don't blame him personally dear. I blame the force that he represents. His beloved APD. The 'Dult police and your YPD paymasters have teamed up to start this phoney war. And your little YPD friend Hanzi is right at the centre of it."

Jem was about to round on Shami when River spoke again.

"Your partner Hanzi is up to his ears in espionage," she said.

"Think," continued River. "Fray's fletch was 'found' in the body of the Kirkless lad. Who murders a rival using an arrow signed with his own runes? Even bargers are not that simple-minded."

"Fray is innocent," agreed Jem. "But why do you think Hanzi is the killer?" demanded Jem, shocked at her mother's accusation.

"I keep an eye on all the spies dear. Your baby-faced partner is what they call a special operative." Jem's jaw dropped. River went on. "Where was little Hanzi when *The Siren* was sunk?"

"He was with me!" snapped Jem. "We watched it sink."

"Bombs can be set with timers. Or set off remotely," said River. Jem shook her head but a look in her eyes gave away her doubts. It was only a micro-expression but her mother read it like a scanner.

"And where was Hanzi the night before? When the Kirkless lad was killed?" she demanded. She filled Jem in on her theory.

"Impossible! Hanzi was with me... On patrol all night," insisted Jem. But as she said the words, she knew it wasn't the truth. Hanzi had slipped off early, saying something about buying a battery.

"Was he really with you ALL night?" asked River. "A little questioning would get to the truth," she suggested.

"Shami left Hanzi for the Kirklesses," said Jem. "So you can put your torturing knives back in your handbag mother."

"Bad Shami!" snapped River. "That action may prove unwise."

Shami's eyes fell. "I had to ditch him," she muttered. Shami had been River's protege in the Father Thames operation. It was like watching a faithful dog waiting for scraps from its mistress. Jem had worked it out long ago. Shami hated Jem, because she secretly wished she was River's daughter. Knowledge of this fuzzy psychology only made Jem resent Shami even more. But here was a new angle. Shami had thrown Hanzi off the boat because she suspected that he was a spy. But who was he spying on? The bargers? The YPD? And what of her mother's second mystery –

the 'big' one? The questions crowded Jem's mind.

"Go ahead and ask Jemima," demanded her mother.

"Alright mother. What's the big secret?" asked Jem flatly.

"Wrong question darling," admonished River. "You should be asking why the YPD and the APD want to start a war between the barger clans? If you'd have come to live with me, I'd have taught you to think logically."

"Why do they want to start a clan war?" asked Jem.

"Because of the evidence I've found – right in the middle of the barger kingdom. They need an excuse to take over the area..."

She was interrupted by a shout from Crow.

"It's the Kirklesses!" croaked the wizened gondolier.

Jem noticed the sky above the ancient boatman. It was only 3pm but it seemed like sunset was coming half a day too soon. The river was bathed in a unusual pinky orange light. Pale clouds scudded above them moving at tremendous speed.

"What now mother?" asked Jem.

"We're leaving," said River. "Old Crow's boat is too fast for a henchman of his advanced years."

"What about Fray and Atticus?" demanded Jem.

"I'm sure your barger friends will die heroic deaths. The singers of the wharves will light bonfires and remember them in song."

Jem drew the tazor and levelled it at her mother.

Shami looked at Jem and settled into a fighting stance.

"Atticus and Fray are the Ferryman's sons," said Jem in desperation. "What will be do when he finds out that you left them for the Kirklesses."

Shami looked at River. Jem knew her barb had found its mark.

"On second thoughts," sighed River, "I've changed my mind."

Shami let out a sigh that River mistook for annoyance.

"A leader has the right to change her mind," said River.

"Small minds place such a high value on consistency. Emerson was right. Consistency is the hobgoblin of the small minded person."

"If the Kirklesses catch us we're going to die. Feel free to quote me on that," said Jem.

The ground began to shake, pitching Jem forward. The air hummed with a continuous vibration

"Relax daughter dearest," said River. "It sounds like those friends of yours have found the ignition."

River crawled up the passage with Jem behind her. They crashed through into the control room, surprising Fray and Atticus.

Atticus lowered his tazor and offered the newcomer a hand.

"Sorry!" he said. "Thought you were dangerous."

When he saw the thin spiderweb of lines on her cheek he slowly raised the gun again.

"She's not dangerous," said Jem. "Although, she is a terrorist."

"I think you mean 'resistance leader' darling," River interjected.

"She's not infectious," added Jem. "So don't worry... much."

Jem turned to her mother and gazed at her with the implacable stare that children reserve for their parents.

"Either of you ever driven a mech?" asked River.

"I had a job loading at the wharf," said Fray.

"No!!!" said Atticus. "Father sacked him for trashing a barge."

"Excellent!" said River. "You'll do perfectly."

Back in the cabin, the red emergency lights had been replaced by a cold white glare. The mech's systems were coming back online.

"Where are we headed?" asked Fray.

"To the Pastkeeper's Palace," said River straightening her hair. "But first we've got to comb out a few Kirkless lice."

Fray settled into the gyroscopic chair. Tiny motors whirred as he familiarised himself with the controls. He extended his arm forwards, rotating it at the elbow. A creaking and whirring noise filled the cabin as the rusted giant responded to his movements.

"Ready?" asked River. Fray smiled and nodded.

"Don't start smashing anything till we're clear," said Jem.

It took five minutes for Shami, River and Jem to join Crow on the gondola. Jem took the rungs three at a time, dropping off the end of the rope ladder and landing on the deck with a crash.

She stumbled for a second time and clutched at the polished wooden rail to steady herself. Her insides needed steadying too.

"Had any good fares recently?" she asked playfully.

"In Kirkless waters?" said Crow seriously, not getting the joke.

"They've spotted us!" cried River.

The idol's eyes glowed red as the motor thrummed. Crow hit the bow thrusters and manoeuvred the prow towards the east. Jem ducked as an unidentified missile whizzed past her ear.

"Why are we heading east?" shouted Jem, her voice lost under the roar of the motor. "Shouldn't we head back to the Ferryman?"

"Indulge me," cooed River. "Sorry Jemima. You'll thank me when all is revealed."

At that moment there was a strangled scream. Crow crashed to the deck like a dead drone.

Jem arrived at the spot where the old barger lay. The fletching of a quarrel was sticking out through his chest. Dark blood was spreading through the material of his coat. Jem's hand was on the shaft, ready to remove it but Shami stopped her.

"No!" she snapped. "It's barbed. You can't remove it like that." A cheer blew over on the wind – Symon Kirkless raised his good fist in triumph. Shouts from the enemy boat confirmed that his dart had found its mark.

Shami put pressure on Crow's chest while Jem tried to bind it. Crimson blood pulsed from the wound. It was useless.

"He's gone," said Jem, letting go of the boatman's lifeless hand.

"Murderers!" yelled Shami towards the Kirkless boat. Jem saw that Shami's eyes had moved from the Kirklesses to her mother. "They'll pay," muttered Shami. But River had already moved on, her hand steady on the tiller as the gondola picked up speed.

Chapter 19: Hit it

Fʀᴀʏ ᴡᴀʟᴋᴇᴅ sᴛᴇᴀᴅɪʟʏ ғᴏʀᴡᴀʀᴅ ɪɴ ᴛʜᴇ ʜᴀʀɴᴇss ᴀɴᴅ ᴛʜᴇ ᴍᴇᴄʜ ʀᴇsᴘᴏɴᴅᴇᴅ, ᴊᴇʀᴋɪʟʏ ᴍɪʀʀᴏʀɪɴɢ ʜɪs ᴍᴏᴠᴇᴍᴇɴᴛs.

"Faster brother! They're getting away," said Atticus.

Fray tried to oblige but the mech lurched to the left with a creak.

"Go forwards – not sideways!" groaned Atticus.

"Shut up!" snapped Fray. "This thing doesn't want to be driven."
The Kirklesses were so busy concentrating on the fleeing gondola that they hadn't noticed the mech. It lurched forwards with surprising speed, its motors whirring, its steel pistons clacking.

Fray worked the controls and the mech swatted at the Kirkless boat. Fantails of water flew up into the air as the mech's iron fist smashed the waves. The blow missed the boat by a good ten metres. But the waves from the mech's punch nearly swamped the Impeacher. Thaddeus whispered soothing nothings to the boat as its exhaust spluttered and its cylinders sucked on unignited fuel.

The mech charged towards its foe like a rusty devil out of hell's deepest hole – its iron limbs raking at the air. Aeson Kirkless flailed back at it, screaming at Thaddeus to get them clear of this infernal machine.

"Hit it boy!" commanded Aeson.

Thaddeus stabbed the starter but the motor only coughed.

"Water in the fuel lines," said Thaddeus pulling a can from his belt. Waves shook the boat as he sprayed propellant into the air intake whilst Symon hit the starter button again and again. The engine turned but it stubbornly refused to start.

The angry mech tore towards the stranded boat. Its immense legs heaving against the pressure of the water. Atticus saw the panic on the Kirklesses' faces. Their mechanic was hammering at his motor with a wrench, spraying the engine with something from a can. Fray waded closer. The Kirkless boat drifted helplessly. Rocking in the harness, Fray made a fist and the mech's mighty hand responded. But before he could unleash the killer blow there was a sickening lurch followed by the squeal of gears and the protest of metal against metal. The mech lost momentum and ground to a standstill.

Chapter 20: Ten count

HANZI STOOD ON THE PLATFORM, LOOKING INTO THE PIGGY EYES OF TYMON KIRKLESS. News of his recapture had spread. The lynch mob had reformed. Hanzi scanned the hostile faces. Then his eyes fixed on the water – it was alive with crocs. A red-faced man was happily stuffing chip coins into his pockets. The YPD had always suspected that the Kirklesses were involved in illegal gaming and Hanzi finally had his proof. Not that it mattered now.

"Hey copper!" called a lanky straw-haired boatman. "Do me a favour…"

"Or he'll jump in there and drown you himself," laughed the man's friend. Tymon Kirkless led Hanzi to the edge of the wharf. Time slowed to a crawl. Hanzi noticed that Tymon's whiskers had been coloured with artificial black dye. As he held up his bound wrists he thought about the vanity of bargers.

Now would be a perfect time for help to arrive, Hanzi thought. But he knew how it worked in the YPD. Perhaps he wasn't an asset worth rescuing? This is what you got if nobody liked you at work. The crowd cheered as Tymon kicked hard, taking Hanzi's legs from under him. He hit the water hard, rolling to right himself, he took a final look up at the lead grey sky. Then he saw three black dots approaching and heard the familiar voice of the drone.

Ten minutes later Hanzi was sitting in the YPD launch on his way to the debriefing. He remembered Jem.

"Did you send someone to pick up Mallard ma'am?" he asked.

Hanzi's boss – Mander Wu – was not a patient person at the best of times. He imagined her glowering at him and shuddered.

"You were told to stay with her," said the voice on the radio.

"The Kirklesses split us up. Mallard came back for me. We were escaping together but a girl in a mask pushed me off the escape boat. They left me for the Kirklesses."

Hanzi didn't get it. Jem had turned up shortly after he'd turned on the transmitter. He'd figured that she'd been dispatched to assist because she was the closest YPD officer to the scene.

"Don't worry ma'am," he said. "Jem doesn't suspect anything."

Chapter 21: Overboard

RIVER HELD A STEADY LINE. The boat was making good progress but they couldn't take anything for granted. The Kirkless's boat was three times as fast as their gondola. "Ready Shami?" she asked, letting go of the throttle for a moment. The gondola slowed to a fast glide as Shami struggled with the task. Jem looked up for the first time in minutes – roused by the slowing engine. Then she saw what Shami was planning.

There was a sudden splash as the bundle slipped over the side. Tears steamed down Jem's face. Then she rounded on her mother.

"Sorry Crow," she sniffed. "You deserved better than this."

"Sorry indeed. But we don't have time to mourn," said River in a voice that was a little too hurried to be soothing.

"Where are we headed?" asked Jem with a note of despair.

"To the Pastkeeper's Palace," said her mother.

"It's closed," sniffed Jem. "Everyone knows that."

"Don't worry dear," said her mother. "They always let me in."

Chapter 22: Out of here

THE ENEMIES GLARED AT EACH OTHER ACROSS THE STRETCH OF WATER. Neither could deal the decisive blow. Fray wrestled in vain with the controls. But the mech had its foot caught in some kind of underwater obstruction. Whatever Fray tried, he could not free it.

"It's not over till it's over," said Atticus, eying the Kirkless's boat It was only a few metres from his mech's grasp. But the platitude died on the robot's cold lips. The air began to hum to the sound of the Kirkless's illegal V8 motor.

Chapter 23: The Palace

Shami was at the helm of the gondola, slipping past sunken hazards and twisted mangroves. She found a channel that took them towards the sunken palace. The idol's lights glowed hot pink. The sun was slipping below the waves. The reflection of the boat's running lights blinked at Jem from an obsidian surface.

"We should have done this sooner," said River taking Jem's hand.

"I came every year with dad," said Jem pulling away. "I expect you were too busy terrorizing people to join us."

River shrugged off the insult.

Wisps of mist kissed the brickwork. Most of the Palace was flooded, of course – it had been so since the Upgrade. But one Mayor had the bright idea of re-opening the upper levels. Once a year the children of the city were let in to inspect what was left of its exhibits. Shami killed the lights as they glided the last metres to the dock. River stepped lightly off the boat, followed by Jem.

"Got everything dear? Backpack? Sandwiches?" asked River.

"Tazor?" added Jem.

River and Jem climbed the stone steps towards the entrance. Shami followed close behind but River stopped her with an upturned palm.

"Stay and watch the boat," she ordered, throwing Shami a radio.

The rain came down in slow waves. Birds fluttered somewhere above. Jem shivered, looking up at the grey archway. The place had a melancholic mausoleum feel, with a dash of the pyramids' faded opulence. The place was full of cracked marble and dead fountains. There was no sign of the famous robots. An inscription above the arch read: 'What's past is prologue.'

"It's a quote from *The Tempest*," said River, who knew it by heart.

"I know," lied Jem. River tutted. She had a mother's nose for untruths. "It's closed," said Jem. "How do we get in? "

River passed her palm slowly over the sensor on the turnstile. When nothing happened, she took out her tazor.

"Come and meet them Jem," said River with a theatrical sweep. "Meet the machines that were going beckon in a new world of leisure time for humanity."

Jem found herself in the centre of a dimly lit hall. From where they stood on the ground level she could make out the mezzanine on the far wall. They passed down the central aisle. River paused to shake hands with a grinning android. Its white plastic paw was extended in friendship.

Jem scanned the vast hall, taking in the terracotta army of cybernetics. From early calculating engines, to assembly line robots with thin insectoid arms, to grinning neo-glass androids.

"Machines to make our cars. To slave in our factories," mused River. The hall seemed to go on forever. Now they were in the construction section where more robots of all sizes stood in ranks.

119

"They would do the lifting, and shifting and slaving," said River. "And what did that leave the humans with?"

Jem snatched a glass from a robot waiter's tray and raised it in mock salute.

"Relaxation?" suggested Jem.

River shook her head. "Brain work," corrected River. "That was the idea. We were courting oblivion Jem. Sleepwalking. We had no more clue what was happening than a lobster in a cooking pot."

"Right now I could do with some artificial intelligence," said Jem, pointing at an exhibit. "You're making my brain hurt."

River shook her head. "Careful what you wish for. In a few decades the dumb machines became cleverer than our brightest scientists.

They were running our hospitals, finances, media. What did the AI's think of their human masters?"

River smiled a thin smile and her cornflower blue eyes sparkled.

"Are you telling me?" began Jem. "That AI's crashed our climate in order to cleanse themselves of the human virus?"

"Don't get too far fetched," said River. "But there's a clue close by."

At the end of the hall was the biggest of the robots, a military droid with sabre arms and a deadly array of auto cannon.

"Combat green! Your favourite colour," remarked River.

"You're not saying that the military droids launched a coup, slaughtered their generals and took over the world?" asked Jem.

Then she saw it – stamped into the robot's chest – alongside a line of multicoloured medal decals. Jem recognised the same logo she'd seen on the Stormfather windfarm and inside the Fray's mech. Two letters inside a globe: G.W. At last, the name came back to her.

At the far edge of the hall, a spiral staircase twisted up to the mezzanine level. Jem pointed at the logo on a farming android.

"Everywhere I go, that logo keeps showing up," she said.

River nodded – a flash of understanding passed over her face.

"Greenwheel S.P.I. When it came to cybernetics, they really were the tip of the lance. The cutting edge."

At top of the winding glass staircase was a balcony. Behind it stood an enormous partition door. The door was built like a tank. In fact it could have been built from a tank because they did a lot of recycling after WW3.

"Now that's what I call a proper door," said Jem, unconsciously using one of her father's expressions.

"It needs to be thick in order to keep the fabbers out," remarked River. Scavengers were always on the hunt for plastic and parts for their fabricating machines.

The walls looked equally serious, made from reinforced concrete.

River rubbed the dust off to reveal shiny white lettering. One by one, letters were revealed. Jem gasped when she read the sign.

"An exhibition about the Climate Upgrade!" gasped Jem. "I thought that the information was lost when the cloud went down."

"The exhibition survived," said River. "The tour usually ends here. But your key will unlock the past."

"What key?" asked Jem.

"The one I left with the Ferryman – didn't he give it to you?"

"Oh THAT key?" replied Jem. River could read her daughter's

eyes. "I gave it to Atticus. He used it to start the mech."

"You entrusted my skeleton key to a kid in a robot mask?" said River.

"That kid is busy holding the Kirklesses off for us," snapped Jem. River rolled her eyes. Jem was put out because it was usually her that did the eye-rolling. "Don't blame me!" she snapped. "If your key was so valuable, why did you leave it with the Ferryman to give to me?"

"It was symbolic," sighed River. "You know — a mother gives her daughter the key to the past and unlocks the future sort of thing..."

"Does the Ferryman know about this exhibition?" asked Jem.

"The Ferryman is a collector. He's only really interested in his masks and relics and such like. Memorabilia."

"How did you come by the key in the first place?" asked Jem.

"A fat man gave it to me," replied River.

"Doesn't he have a spare?" asked Jem.

"I don't know. I'd love ask him. But your YPD friend blasted him with a tazor. Remember?"

Jem fought to put the sad memory aside. Nick had shot the Fatman trying to bust out of Father Thames' lab. Before she could reply to her mother, there was a rush of air and a metallic voice rang out.

Jem eyed the metal sphere suspiciously and turned to River.

"I'm not sure I can handle this," Jem said. "The last time a drone ordered me to leave the area, it ended badly."

"What kind of badly?" asked River.

"Rats and blood sacks," shuddered Jem. "You don't want to know."

The drone whirred and descended towards them. Jem took a step back from the rail.

"Leave immediately," it demanded. "The museum is closed!"

"Museum?" said Jem. "I thought this was a palace."

"Follow me!" said River, turning her back on the drone and scrambling for the radio on her belt. She wound it up to charge it and put it to her ear.

"I can't get through to Shami," she moaned. "The walls are too thick."

"Where to now?" asked Jem.

"I'm worried about your education," said River, striding back down the glass stairs. "We are going to get that key so we can get through

125

the door and into the exhibition."

Jem struggled to keep pace with her mother. Their spherical metal friend was hovering just behind them. Now they were doing what it wanted – leaving – it had fallen silent.

At the bottom of the stairs, River tried the radio again. Jem looked out across the chamber and shivered.

"These old robots creep me out," she said. "It's as if they are all going to come alive or something."

Hostile red eyes glared at them from the long shadows.

River regarded the boy in the robot mask with a nonchalant calm.

"Just the robot we were looking for," she said. "Where's Fray with that mech of yours?"

"It was too big to fit through the door," said the robot. "We didn't want to trash this place."

River laughed. "Don't worry – you've got permission."

"Break down the walls if you have too," commanded River. "But get it in here fast."

"We need the key to the mech," explained Jem.

River glared at Aeson Kirkless, not intimidated by the cold blue eyes glaring back at her from under the wide brim of his hat.

Jem saw the truth of that. The hall was teeming with Kirklesses armed with fletchettes and shuriken. It looked like the whole clan was here.

River's tazor lashed Tymon with a whip of blue sparks. The big man dropped like a wrecked car from a scrap yard magnet.

Jem coughed. The air was filled with the acrid note of burning hair. Tymon groaned and clutched at his chest. River must have modified her tazor – thought Jem. It was far more powerful than a YPD weapon.

"Down!" cried River, pulling Jem to safety as a volley of darts came towards them. Jem's eyes met her mother's. She talked in whispers with Atticus and pointed down the hall.

"I'll draw their fire," said the boy in the robot mask. A few seconds later he poked his head above the exhibit and the air was thick with darts and missiles again. After counting four seconds, River and Jem leapt up and took off down the pathway, weaving left and right to make themselves harder to hit. Jem grabbed her mother's hand, pulling her to a standstill by the military droid they'd seen earlier.

There was a bright pulsing flash followed by a billow of smoke. The eyes of Atticus's robot mask glowered through the gloom.

"Smoke grenades," he said. "I've only got a couple."

"Quick," said Jem "There's not much time."

Atticus clambered up the shoulders of the droid and perched on its square shoulder, clinging onto a line of auto cannon to steady himself. Removing the mask – he strapped it to the droid's face and climbed back down.

"Good job you brought the remote," said Jem.

Atticus held a tiny microphone between his fingers.

"What do I say?" asked Atticus.

"Anything! Threaten them," suggested Jem.

"Threatening folks with words is not my style," called Atticus.

Chapter 24: Override

SYMON KIRKLESS CAME TO A HALT WHEN HE HEARD THE COMMAND...

Even by the brutal standards of military droids, the Shabbet Systems Warhog was a big ugly robot. If Symon Kirkless had noticed the pile of dusty brochures next to the exhibit he'd have known it was ugly on the inside too. It had aggression sensors, auto cannon, gas grenades and if you bought the options pack – phosphor bombs and a 'baby' nuke. As well as battlefield weaponry, it came with a full range of crowd pacification gear. Symon had no idea it was harmless and deactivated.

"What do I say now?" asked Atticus.

"Just keep threatening them," Jem replied.

"Er... Like...halt or I'll have to shoot you dead!" boomed the speakers in the mask. The techs had given it a bassy voice that exuded authority and an amplifier to match. The sound hit Symon like a smack in the face. He eyed the metal giant suspiciously.

"Don't fire," he pleaded, extending his palms. "Look! I'm dropping my weapon just like you said."

"Cool," said the war machine. "I mean, thanks for your cooperation!" But Aeson Kirkless wasn't born yesterday.

Moving surprisingly fast for a man with a metal blade instead of a foot, Aeson Kirkless strode towards the giant robot with his head held high. He looked for all the world as if he alone was about to smite the metal fiend and send it back to the pit. The rest of his clan drew strength from him and came creeping out of the shadows.

"Stop!" yelled Atticus into the mic. War is deception, but the trick had been spotted. The booming voice had lost its authority.

"What now?" cried Jem, rounding on her mother.

"Run?" suggested Atticus, peeking out from his hiding place.

"The key," said River. "We need the key from the mech, remember?"

At that moment, the ground beneath their feet began to shake. Clouds of dust sent the Kirklesses scattering like startled gulls.

Fray swung his arm in an arc, rocking in the mech's control harness. The mech's massive arm responded, scattering Kirkless goons like ducks in a bread storm. Fray strode forward, with Aeson Kirkless in his sights. Aeson dodged the blow but he tripped and the fall knocked the wind out of him. One well-placed foot would crush his skull like an eggshell. Without hesitation, Fray raised his right leg. His metal proxy responded, its limb raised for the kill.

"Release her," called Atticus. "We'll trade her for your uncle."
Symon wasn't used to making decisions. He shifted on his feet and looked to the remaining Kirklesses for support. Tymon glared at River, remembering the pain of her tazor blast. They both looked at Aeson but the old monster was too stunned to speak. Finally Symon nodded, waving the others back.

"Easy now!" said Symon, edging forward towards his uncle.

There were only a few metres between Symon and Uncle Aeson. The mech had gone eerily quiet – its motor powered down to conserve energy. Slowly Jem and Atticus edged towards the ladder by the mech's right leg. They could see Shami – still masked, her hands restrained behind her back. Symon took a step towards his uncle.

"Stay where you are Kirkless," boomed Fray from high up in the mech. "Wait till my brother gets to you. Then we'll do the exchange."

Symon waited patiently, like seconds at a duel. At last Jem made it to the mech's leg. Fray lowered a rope ladder.

"Inside!" said Atticus. "You go first, I'll follow with Shami."

Jem nodded and began to climb the rope ladder, conscious of the many weapons aimed at her back. When she reached the top, Atticus was ready for the prisoner exchange.

"You don't get your uncle till Shami and I are up in the mech," said Atticus.

A few minutes later, it was over. Symon had his uncle back and Jem and Atticus were safe in the cab of the mech. Shami was the last to come through the door, banging her head as she stooped through the hatchway. Jem saw it first. Something in the way the masked figure moved. She reached for her tazor, but it was too late...

"What are you doing Shami?" cried Jem, not seeing who was really behind Shami's mask.

"Kirkless?!" gasped Atticus, reaching for the wrench at his side.

"This is for my kin," said Thaddeus. The muzzle of his tazor flashed. Fray's body twitched in the harness, and the mech rocked wildly from side to side. Stomping back down the hall towards the back of the hanger. The sudden movement saved Atticus. Thaddeus's tazor blast missed him and dissipated into the Plexiglas screen. Atticus swung the wrench but Thaddeus was too quick, ducking the blow with ease. Atticus was over extended. With frightening speed Thaddeus's boot kicked out, smashing the weapon from Atticus' gloved hand. A flat-handed blow took the disarmed barger on the temple. As he fell to his knees, Thaddeus turned his attentions to Jem – a little squeeze of the eyes registering his recognition.

Jem looked at Thaddeus's tazor. It was some kind of custom model with a black muzzle shaped like a snake's hood. Thaddeus had a clear shot. Seconds slipped past. Why didn't he fire? Then she realised. His last shot had drained the tazor. There was enough juice to stun but not to kill. He was waiting for his battery to recover.

Jem scanned the cabin for options. There was no way out of the except the hatchway where the barger stood. Fray had stopped moving now. He lay slumped in the harness. Through the dirty Plexiglas screen, Jem made out the familiar figure of her mother. River had made her way back up the spiral stairs and now she stood on the balcony looking down on the mech. She was waving frantically from the balcony across a ten metre divide.

As soon as the plan popped into Jem's mind she executed it. When hunting for the starter, Jem had noticed the canopy release lever. It was protected by a transparent plastic cover. Ducking as low as possible, Jem leaped for the mech's controls and removed the cover. She heard Thaddeus cursing her and smelt the distinctive smell of plasma as the tazor discharged. But her hand was already on the lever as the sparks railed towards her. With a gasp, she pulled the lever and the explosive bolts fired. The window pane was blasted out of the cabin. Part of the tazor blast had hit Jem's right leg. The pain was searing. Jem gasped. She knew she was in trouble. Thaddeus stared at the weapon, waiting for it to recover again. Through a mist of pain Jem could clearly make out what her mother was saying.

"I'm kind of busy in here mother," called Jem over her shoulder through gritted teeth. The vast hall sucked the sarcasm from her voice.

"The key!" demanded River. "I'll throw it back as soon as the door starts opening."

The silence was excruciating, but not as excruciating as the pain from her wounded leg. There was precious little time to think. Thaddeus was eying the key, clearly with his own ideas. He crossed the space in two long strides and lunged for the key. Jem was just ahead of him. She wrenched the key free from the ignition and sent it arcing through the void where the cabin window had been.

River caught the key easily, casually acknowledging Jem's accurate throw as if she was watching a marsh cricket match on a Sunday.

"Help!" called Jem.

Thaddeus eyed her with a grim expression. The barger was slight and wiry – the runt of the Kirkless litter. He had inherited none of the Kirkless muscle – but he'd got a fine helping of Uncle Aeson's temper.

Boiling over, he ditched the dead tazor and rushed at Jem with his fists flailing. Jem stepped sideways to avoid his charge. In his fury, Thaddeus didn't spot Atticus' boot come up to trip him. Jem exhaled, fighting the pain from her leg. Then she heard Thaddeus's final scream. The momentum of his charge had taken him through the glassless window to the concrete floor below.

From her position on the balcony, River heard the commotion following Thaddeus's fall. Now she stood before the armoured partition door looking for a sensor. There was no sensor but on the right of the keypad was a slot marked 'overide'. River inserted the key and twisted. A metallic voice rang out...

The armoured door began to rise, its ancient motor purring. River let out a curse and removed the key, ready to dash back to Jem's aid. But the joy died on her lips. As soon as the key was out, the door began to close again.

The speaker taunted her with the confirmation:

"Override key removed."

Cursing – River rushed back to the balcony with the key in her hand..

Yelling to get Jem's attention, River took a coil of rope from her backpack and threw it in a looping arc. Jem caught it easily. The second package – a black plastic tube was a harder catch, as it came in faster.

"What now?" called Jem, stealing a look down at the Kirklesses.

Jem shuddered. The tube had come to a rest by Fray's lifeless foot. His body swayed in the harness as she retrieved the tube, removing the lid to reveal the zip wire harness rig.

"Heights!" thought Jem. "Why does it always have to be heights?" She tried to command her foot to get into the harness but it was a battle – the muscles of her lower right leg were still burning from the tazor blast. It was a struggle to limp, let alone swing.

"Here!" said Atticus, moving forward to assist her.

Jem felt a pang of guilt. She might be able to swing out of here – but what about poor Atticus? She couldn't leave the barger in the mech

– with the body of his brother slowly cooling and swan off with her mother to solve a mystery.

"I'll manage," said Jem.

Atticus grabbed a box with a green letter M on it. Rushing, he turned out the contents. A laugh of triumph confirmed that he'd found what he was after. Jem saw the two hypodermic vials of pain killing medicine.

"Two derms," said Atticus. "One for you and one for me."

"Is this medicine still good?" asked Jem suspiciously.

"Only one way to find out," said Atticus – jabbing the derm into her left leg. Almost instantly the calm began to bloom through her searing muscles. She sighed with relief.

"Come on then," said Atticus, helping her into the zip wire harness. Ignoring her protests, he checked the rope. Jem attached a second, thinner length of twine to the harness.

"What's that for?" asked Atticus.

"To send the rig back," said Jem. "So you can come back after me."

"Go!" whispered Atticus.

Jem felt the rush of air on her face and heard the whine of the zip wire rig on the taut rope. It was a short glide. She came in fast, nearly smashing her good leg against the balcony as she landed near River.

Her mother clutched a dark metal sphere. Smiling she hurled it at the Kirklesses. A plume of dark smoke bloomed from the hall below.

"What was that?" coughed Jem.

"Gas grenade," said River, throwing another down the spiral stairs. Jem didn't ask. Her mother packed gas grenades in her bag in the same way that other mothers pack lipstick.

"What is it?" asked River, noticing Jem's bleak expression.

River nodded but the name didn't register.

"The boy in the robot mask!" Jem snapped.

"Don't worry.," said River, helping Jem unclip herself from the zip wire. "Bargers grow up tough. He'll be fine."

"They killed Fray," sobbed Jem, the tears coming faster now.

Once again, the name didn't register with her mother.

"Fray was Atticus's brother," she said, her voice thick with grief.

"Why?" demanded Jem.

"The Climate Upgrade," said River. "The truth is behind that door."

"So I just run off? Sorry Atticus, I'm leaving you to die. We have a mystery to solve."

Tears ran down Jem's face as she rounded on River. She reeled off the roll call of casualties in her mother's environmental war.

"Old Crow is dead. Fray is dead. And I never thought I'd hear myself saying this. But goodness knows what's happened to your little friend Shami. Or have you written her off too?"

"They killed the planet Jem," said River. "Millions died when the Climate Upgrade failed. And they are still using 'the environment' as an excuse to keep us meek and servile. To obey their laws."

As Jem was about to answer, a shape appeared through the fog at the top of the staircase. Raising a fist, it cried out.

River grabbed Jem's arm and dragged her away, throwing her last smoke bomb at Aeson's bladed foot. Jem heard it hiss as they reached the closed door. River inserted the key and turned it clockwise.

"Override key inserted," blared the electronic voice and the obedient door began to rise up on its rollers.

"Quickly Jem!" ordered River, trying to bundle Jem through the crack at the bottom of the opening door.

The beam of River's torch slid over an enormous sign suspended from the high ceiling. It read: Climate 2.0 – sponsored by Greenwheel S.P.I. River let out a triumphant laugh. The roller door was fully open now. Still standing inside the hanger, River reached through and removed the key. The door began to close. "Come on Jem!" she called. "The answers are waiting."

"Who are you staying for?" asked River coolly. "For poor Shami?" She let out a cruel laugh. "I'm not so sure she'll be pleased to see you, without me by your side."

The door slid slowly down again, its electric motors whirring.

"Or is it your little barger boy?" laughed River incredulously.

"His name is Atticus," snapped Jem.

"You don't get it," began Jem. "It's not YOUR decision. You don't get to decide if I stay or go, mother."

Before River could answer, Jem ducked under the closing door – back to where the Kirklesses were waiting.

"Is one barger worth saving?" yelled her mother from behind the iron curtain.

The skeletal figure of Aeson Kirkless loomed out of the mist like an avenging wraith. In one hand he held Atticus' mask, still smoking from the blast. His finger extended accusingly towards Jem.

Jem dropped to her knees as the fletches whistled towards her. Screaming she rolled for the closing door. The Kirklesses let loose with everything they had. Darts and fletches pinged off the armoured wall. The shock of an impact knocked the key out of Jem's hand.

Time slowed to a halt as Jem rolled. She was too late – she thought. Too late to get her body through the narrowing gap of the closing door. She would be pinned by the door like a vice. Her legs slid though first but she was stuck. Her mother had hold of her boots and was trying to drag her to safety. But it was hopeless. She was jammed solid. In a few moments the Kirklesses would have a knife at her throat.

Stinging smoke forced Jem's eyes closed. And when she opened them, she heard a familar voice.

"Shami?" said Jem. "They had your mask. I thought you were dead."
"No talking Mallard," Shami replied.

Shami raised her tazor and let off a couple of vicious blasts at the Kirklesses. Jem saw that Shami had wedged the door with a metal pole and was frantically trying to lever it up to free Jem.

Gradually the opposing forces shifted, breaking the equilibrium. Jem slid free from the door's pinch and felt her mother's gloved hands hauling her though the gap.

"Wait Shami!" called Jem, recoiling from her mother's touch. "She doesn't care about you. She doesn't care about anyone..."

"I care," said Shami. Now the obstruction was clear, the door was closing. Jem sensed the cruel hand of the inevitable in the way the door slid shut, leaving Shami with the Kirklesses.

Blinking, Jem looked up and went back to the door. It was warm to the touch from the tazor blasts that had been fired. There was no sound from coming from the other side.

"Come with me," said River, pressing a white mask into Jem's shaking hand.

"Why?" demanded Jem, trying to suppress her sobs.

To be continued... in *London Stars*

The *London Deep* series

London Deep is set in the future in a flooded London where rival police forces for youth and grown ups compete to keep the peace.

London Deep (Book 1)
ISBN: 9781906132033 £7.99

Father Thames (Book 2)
ISBN: 9781906132040 £7.99

Threadneedle (Book 3)
ISBN: 9781906132057 £7.99

London Sink (Book 4)
ISBN: 9781906132378 £8.99

London Stars (Book 5)
ISBN: 9781906132569 £8.99

www.londondeep.co.uk

Book I: *London Deep*

Jemima Mallard is having a bad day. First she loses her air,
then someone steals her houseboat, and now the Youth Cops
think she's mixed up with a criminal called Father Thames. Not
even her dad, a Chief Inspector with the 'Dult Police, can help
her out this time. Oh – and London's been underwater ever
since the Climate Upgrade.

ISBN: 978-1-906132-03-3 £7.99

Concept and story by Robin Price. Artwork by Paul McGrory.

Chosen as a 'Recommended Read' for World Book Day 2011.
One of the *Manchester Book Award's* 24 recommended titles for 2010.

Book II: *Father Thames*

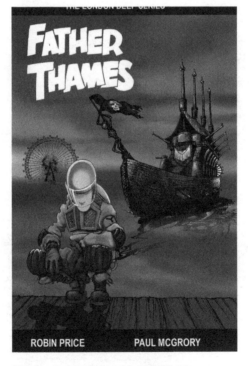

ISBN: 9781906132040   £7.99

"With non-stop adrenalin-fuelled drama throughout it won't disappoint both new and existing ardent fans of the London Deep series. The mix of text and graphic novel art-work throughout the book adds a further level to the story."
– LOVE READING

Book III: *Threadneedle*

ISBN: 9781906132057   £7.99

Story by Robin Price. Artwork by Paul McGrory.

Book IV: *London Sink*

ISBN: 9781906132378   £8.99
Story by Robin Price. Artwork by Rebecca Davy.

Book V: *London Stars*

In the thrilling final instalment of the series - Jemima Mallard finally discovers the truth behind the Climate Upgrade that flooded London.

London Stars (Book 5)
ISBN: 9781906132569 £8.99

Available Autumn 2019. Artwork by Rebecca Davy.

ALSO BY ROBIN PRICE...

The Spartapuss series is set in ancient Rome, in a world ruled by cats.

I AM SPARTAPUSS
BOOK I

Spartapuss, a ginger cat, is happy managing Rome's most famous Bath & Spa. But Fortune has other plans for him.
ISBN: 978-1-9061324-2-2

CATLIGULA
BOOK II

When Catligula becomes Emperor, his madness brings Rome to within a whisker of disaster.
ISBN: 978-1-9061324-8-4

DIE CLAWDIUS
BOOK III

The Emperor Clawdius decides to invade Spartapuss' home – The Land of the Kitons.

ISBN: 978-0-9546576-8-0

BOUDICAT
BOOK IV

Queen Boudicat has declared war on Rome and she wants Spartapuss to join her rebel army.
ISBN: 978-190-61320-1-9

CLEOCATRA'S KUSHION
BOOK V

Spartapuss must travel through Fleagypt to the land of the Kushites and find his missing son.
ISBN: 97819-061326-7-5

BEOWUFF
AND THE
HOrrid HEN

Viking dog Beowuff is all bark and no bite, a disgrace to the memory of his fierce ancestors.

Banished from his homeland, Beowuff finds himself ship-wrecked on a troubled island. Its King needs a champion. His hall is under attack from the hideous Hendel – an evil chicken of monstrous proportions.

ISBN: 9781906132385

UK £7.99

"My husband, professor Burns-Longship has made a second incredible find! This time there are dragon-dogs involved! Surely now the experts in Scandinavia will return my calls!"
– Mrs Burns-Longship, The Village Blog.

Beowuff might sound familiar
to history lovers, because his character echoes the ancient hero Beowulf (1000 A.D.), who appears in one of the earliest recorded poems in Old English.

www.mogzilla.co.uk • info@mogzilla.co.uk

London Deep reviews

One of the *Manchester Book Award's* 24 recommended reads 2010 and a Recommended Read for World Book Day 2011.

'This is a terrifically atmospheric page-turning adventure told through words and comic art... it's a rattling good read and one in which you are sure to be drawn in to Jemima's exploits of survival.' – *Lovereading.co.uk*

'Robin Price's writing is quirky with a bit of an edge to it that greatly adds realism to this dystopian version of London... Add in the gritty illustrated comic panels by Paul McGrory and you find this is indeed something quite new, not only in plot, but in style... Children aged 9 and above who are reluctant to read but love comics will find the shorter full text sections easy to get through, with the comic panels adding punctuation to the action occurring within that part of the chapter.' – *Dooyoo.co.uk*

'Is this part graphic novel, part standard text, or is it a story with illustrations...? ... My eleven year old loved it and seemed to have no trouble cutting backwards and forwards between the two...' – Rachel Ayers Nelson, *School Librarian Magazine*

'Through pace and narrative power, both admirably sustained, the book avoids becoming didactic. This is no campaign document on climate change... The characterization, especially of Jemima and Nick, is forceful and convincing. They capture the reader's interest and carry the narrative forward...' – *Armadillo Magazine*

www.londondeep.co.uk